To My Dear Daughter 4.95
Aynsley.

Love Forever,
Your Mom.
♡

A Made-over
Chelsea

D0964149

Best Friends

#7

A Made-over Chelsea

Hilda Stahl

CROSSWAY BOOKS • WHEATON, ILLINOIS
A DIVISION OF GOOD NEWS PUBLISHERS

Dedicated with love to
Cathy Runyon

A Made-over Chelsea.

Copyright © 1992 by Word Spinners, Inc.

Published by Crossway Books, a division of
Good News Publishers, 1300 Crescent Street, Wheaton, Illinois 60187.

Cover illustration: Paul Casale

First printing, 1992

Printed in the United States of America

ISBN 0-89107-683-2

Contents

1

First Day of School

Chelsea McCrea stood in front of the full-length mirror in her bedroom. Giant tears welled up in her blue eyes and traced a path down her freckles. "How can I go to school looking like this?" She was way too ordinary-looking. She frowned and peered closer at herself. Actually she was almost ugly. With a groan she whirled away from the mirror and rubbed her hands down her peach-colored slacks and tugged at the neckline of her white-and-peach pullover top. Why had her new outfit looked so beautiful yesterday and so awful today? She'd been so sure it was the perfect thing to wear for the first day of school that she hadn't even asked the Best Friends, Hannah Shigwam, Roxie Shoulders, and Kathy Aber, about it.

"I should've asked them!" Chelsea flung back her mass of red hair and then impatiently wiped away her tears. They knew how middle-school kids dressed here in Middle Lake, Michigan. She only knew about middle school in Benson, Oklahoma. Why hadn't she thought of that yesterday afternoon when the Best Friends had come over for a visit? Impatiently she opened her closet and rifled through the row of dresses, blouses, skirts, and pants. Maybe the jeans she'd bought a couple of days ago would be better than the pleated dress pants. Or maybe the flowered dress. Or her blue denim skirt and short-sleeved red top.

With a cry she slammed the closet door. She'd wear what she had on. Today she'd see what everyone else was wearing and then dress accordingly tomorrow.

"Oh, I don't want to go to school today!"

She jerked open her bedroom door and peered out into the hallway. Was Rob as nervous as she was? He was going into seventh grade, one grade above her. Before moving here he'd been too shy to speak to any stranger. Now, after a summer of no computer and working a job, he was more outgoing. He already knew he'd be in the Computer Club in the middle school.

From his room eight-year-old Mike was singing at the top of his lungs. He was in second grade and a pro in gymnastics. He was a lot like Dad—he made friends easily, was never afraid of new places or things, and was always on the lookout for a new adventure.

"Mike, hurry so you can feed Gracie," Mom called from the bottom of the stairs. Gracie was Ezra Menski's dog. He was on a honeymoon with his new wife, Roxie's grandmother. Smells of coffee and scrambled eggs drifted from downstairs.

"Be right there, Mom."

Chelsea quickly closed the door. A warm September breeze ruffled the curtains at the windows. The sun brightened the mauve-and-blue bedspread. She heard Mike run past her door. She wasn't ready for Mike's excitement about taking care of Gracie or about the first day of school.

Chelsea looked longingly at her phone. Maybe she should call Hannah or Roxie or Kathy and ask what they were wearing. She glanced at her watch and shook her head. They'd be rushing around just like she was.

With one last worried look in the mirror, Chelsea walked from her room and down the hall to Rob's. She knocked. "Rob, it's me."

"Come in." His voice was muffled.

Chelsea opened the door and stood in the doorway. Rob sat on his carefully made bed, his head in his hands. He wore jeans and a tan-and-green shirt. His auburn hair was mussed, and his sneakers weren't tied. "You'd better hurry, Rob."

"I thought I could make it today without being scared." He jumped up and spread his hands wide. "I feel like I'm going to throw up!"

"You say that the first day of school every year."

"But this year I really mean it." Rob pressed his hand against his flat stomach and groaned.

Chelsea giggled. "Oh, Rob, how are we going to make it in school today?"

Rob groaned again. "I wish we were back in Oklahoma!" He brushed his hair and tied his sneakers. "No, I guess I don't."

"I like it here too." She hadn't thought she would. But the Best Friends had made living here exciting and fun.

Rob walked toward his door. "Maybe I'm just hungry. Let's have breakfast, then see."

Sighing, Chelsea walked down the hall and then side by side with Rob down the stairs. She and Rob were as close to being best friends as a brother and sister could be. "I wish we were in the same class—then we could hang out together."

"Join the Computer Club. Sixth graders are allowed in there."

Chelsea wrinkled her nose as she slid her hand down the smooth, shiny rail. "Computers are too boring."

"Not to me."

Chelsea stepped into the kitchen. Gracie barked outside the back door on the deck. Mom set plates with scrambled eggs and toast on the table. Her shoulder-length red hair was combed neatly back from her oval face. A long pink blouse hung over her black slacks. She smiled, and her blue eyes lit up.

"Chelsea, you look beautiful!"

Chelsea dropped her head. "Don't say that! Am I too dressed up for school?"

"Not at all!" Mom kissed Chelsea's pale cheek and then hugged Rob. "Sit down and eat. You have only a few minutes before you leave to catch the bus." All the kids from the subdivision, The Ravines, met the school bus on the street outside the housing development.

Chelsea managed to eat most of her eggs and half her toast. She drank her milk, then wiped her mouth with a white paper napkin. "Mom, should I wear jeans?"

"You don't have time to change anyway. Wear 'em tomorrow if you want."

Laughing, Mike ran in. "Mom, can we get a dog? I want one so bad!"

"No dog, Mike. Sit and eat. But wash your hands first." Mom tossed Mike a towel. "And hurry."

Chelsea brushed a crumb off her pullover. What could she do to get Mom to let her stay home?

"Here's a Scripture for you today." Mom opened the Bible to the marker. "Psalm 34:15. 'The eyes of the Lord are upon the righteous, and his ears are open unto their cry.'" Mom smiled. "God is always watching and listening to you to help you. You're never alone! Remember that when it seems like you are."

"Thanks, Mom," Rob said, sounding relieved.

Chelsea thought about the verse as she ran outdoors with Rob and Mike. She looked next door to see if Roxie was still home, but she was already gone. So was Hannah from across the street.

A few minutes later Chelsea reached the crowd of

kids just as the bus pulled up, its brakes hissing. She caught a glimpse of Hannah, but she was making sure her eight-year-old twin sisters and her nine-year-old sister were getting on the bus. Chelsea looked around for Roxie but couldn't find her in the mob. Maybe she was already on the bus. Yesterday Hannah and Roxie had said they'd save a seat for Chelsea. She stepped into the bus, stood in the crowded aisle, and looked around for them. Suddenly someone shoved her, and she plopped down into an empty seat. She tried to get up so she could look for the Best Friends, but the stream of kids rushing down the aisle kept pushing her back into her seat, so she stayed there. The bus smelled like diesel and grape chewing gum. Two little girls sat on the seat with Chelsea. She said hi, but they didn't even look at her.

At long last the bus lurched and pulled away from the curb. Chelsea locked her hands in her lap and looked straight ahead. She was sooo nervous. The two girls who shared the seat with her chattered just like Kathy's little sister Megan did. The noise of all the voices pounded against Chelsea's head. Her heart thundered in her ears. She bit her lip and tried to relax.

Several minutes later the bus stopped at the middle school, and the boys and girls began streaming out. Suddenly Chelsea spotted the Best Friends—and they saw her! The crowd was between them, but Kathy shouted, "Chelsea! Meet us by the Student Common—take a left, then a right as soon as you get into the school."

A few minutes later Chelsea finally got out of the bus. Her legs trembled as she looked at the three-story brick building. A large grassy lawn stretched out in front of it, and a huge paved parking area sat on the side. Tall maple trees shaded the lawn and the building.

Slowly Chelsea walked into the school. She sort of knew her way around because Mom had brought her in to enroll her a few days earlier. Had Kathy said to take a left, then a right or a right, then a left? She knew her homeroom was on the second floor, but she wanted to see the Best Friends first. Before long she knew she was lost and had no idea of how to get to the Student Common—or even her homeroom! In the mass of students she tried to find someone she knew from church, but they all looked like strangers. No one spoke to her. They all acted like she was invisible. Would she do that to a new student?

As she walked she tried to think back to last year and her school in Oklahoma, but she couldn't remember a single new student there. Well, if there had been one, she'd have welcomed her and shown her around!

When she finally found her homeroom, she was late. Late on her very first day! She sat in a chair in the back row, the classroom's last empty seat. The sun shone through windows lining one side of the room. Maps hung on a wall. The teacher's desk seemed small compared to the blackboard behind it. Chelsea saw Hannah sitting up toward the front, but she didn't look back and didn't see Chelsea. Roxie was chattering with two girls, so she didn't see Chelsea either. Chelsea chewed her bottom lip. Kathy was talking with Justine, one of the girls she practiced cheerleading with. Chelsea sank lower in her seat. Had they really not seen her, or were they mad because she hadn't met them at the Student Common like they'd asked her to? Would the Best Friends drop her now that they were back in school with all their old friends?

Her hands icy, Chelsea slowly looked around the stuffy room full of chattering students. Most of the girls were dressed like she was. A few wore jeans and a few skirts. Most of the boys wore jeans, but a few had on dress pants.

Chelsea sighed heavily. If she were back in Oklahoma, she'd be sitting with Sidney and talking a mile a minute. She'd never had a first day of school without a friend beside her until now. Tears stung the backs of her eyes, but she quickly blinked them away. It would be too humiliating to cry.

Finally a man walked to the desk in front of the room and stood until everyone grew silent. He was medium build with gray hair in a crew cut. His navy-blue suit fit too snugly across his shoulders. "I'm Mr. Borgman, and I'm your homeroom, reading, social studies, and English teacher." His voice was deep and gravelly.

He talked on and on until Chelsea's head hurt. How could she remember everything he said? She glanced at her watch. Only fifteen minutes had passed! Could she survive an entire day?

A million years later, at lunchtime, Chelsea desperately looked for the Best Friends in the noisy, crowded hallway. She knew there were split lunchtimes, but she had thought all of the students in her homeroom shared the same lunchtime. Maybe she was wrong—there was no sign of the Best Friends anywhere. Would she have to eat alone? That would be awful. She was in a room full of strangers. Her stomach cramped. The noise beat against her eardrums.

Just then someone tugged on her hair. She glanced over her shoulder. A girl she hadn't noticed before stood there grinning at her. The girl had a mass of blonde curls held high on her head in a lime-green clip. She wore lime-green shorts over bright orange tights. Her lime, orange, and purple short-sleeved top barely covered her waist.

The girl giggled. "Hi. You new?"

Chelsea nodded. "I'm Chelsea McCrea . . . from Oklahoma."

"Cute accent. I'm Kesha Bronski . . . from everywhere. I was born in New Jersey, but I don't remember that." Kesha giggled again. "Want to eat together?"

Chelsea sighed in relief. "Yes! I hate eating alone."

"Yeah, I know what you mean." Kesha pushed through the crowded doorway and into the cafeteria.

Chelsea hesitated, then followed her. Smells of fried fish, pizza, and something Chelsea couldn't identify made her stomach lurch. Students pushed and shouted. Rock music blasted over all the other noises.

"Stay close and I'll get us food and a table," Kesha said over her shoulder as she walked to the line and cut in.

Flushing, Chelsea followed. She'd never taken cuts before.

"That's the only way to get in before the best food's gone," Kesha said, giggling.

Without looking around, Chelsea chose pizza and a can of apple juice. She didn't want to see the angry looks or hear the ugly remarks of the kids behind them. She hurried after Kesha.

Kesha stopped at a table where two boys sat. Each table had room for eight people.

"This table's saved," the boy with a black shirt said.

"Too bad." Kesha sat down.

Chelsea wanted to run from the room.

Kesha motioned to her tray of food as she scowled at the boys. "You guys even touch my tray, I'll send you flying across the room."

Chelsea gasped. Did she really want to sit with Kesha?

"Sit down, Chel Sea." She said it loud, and when Kesha said her name it sounded like Chel Sea. "Sit down and eat."

Flushing, Chelsea dropped to a chair. Without looking at the boys, she ate her slice of pizza and drank her apple juice. She almost choked on the juice. It was lukewarm and sour tasting.

Kesha ate her fish sandwich and french fries quickly, then leaned close to Chelsea. "Don't you hate being treated like the Invisible Woman?"

"How'd you know I felt like that?" Chelsea asked in surprise.

"I know how *I* felt. But now when I go to a new school I know how to dress and act so people *know* I'm around. You should do the same thing."

Chelsea thought about it a while. "I don't know . . . I'm not that brave."

"Do you want every day to be like today?"

"No!"

"Then do what I do, Chel Sea! You'll be glad you did. Where d' ya live?"

Chelsea told her.

"Sure, I know The Ravines. I'll come see you after school and help you pick out the right thing for you to wear tomorrow."

Chelsea hesitated. One of Mom's rules when she or Dad wasn't home was that no one could go in the house—especially not a stranger. Kesha was definitely a stranger—and strange! Chelsea's pulse fluttered. Mom wouldn't be home until 6, so Kesha could stop by without Mom even knowing. "Can you come right after school?"

"Sure. I'll ride the bus with you."

Chelsea's eyes widened. She'd heard the bus rules. One of them was no one could ride a bus he/she didn't belong on without written permission. "Can you do that?"

"I can do anything I want." Kesha giggled and bumped Chelsea's shoulder. "Before you know it, you can too."

Chelsea nodded and smiled. She'd try anything to keep from feeling invisible the rest of the school year. Kesha was going to be a good friend.

With her head up but her stomach knotted, Chelsea walked to math class with Kesha.

2

Best Friends

Chelsea glanced all around the yard to make sure no one was looking. No one was, and she breathed easier. Mike and Rob were already inside the house. Rob probably was working on his computer, and Mike was changing his clothes so he could play with the dog. The boys hadn't noticed Kesha or they would've asked about her. And even if they had seen her, they'd never dream Chelsea would let Kesha inside the house without their parents being there.

"What are you waiting for?" Kesha asked with a giggle.

"Nothing." Chelsea opened the front door and let Kesha step in first, then followed her. She closed the door quickly. The bowl of potpourri made the hall smell like apples and cinnamon.

Kesha looked around. She touched the grandfather clock and the large fern. She peeked into the living room and looked up the open stairs. "Nice place."

"Thanks. My room's upstairs." Trembling,

Chelsea hurried on up, with Kesha slowly following behind. Chelsea led Kesha into her room and quickly closed the door.

"Wow!" Kesha stood in the middle of the room and slowly turned all the way around. "Double wow!"

Chelsea opened her closet, but Kesha paid no attention. She just rubbed her hand over the iron-and-brass bedstead, touched the mauve-and-blue bedspread, lifted the phone off the hook, set it back, then looked at herself in the mirror. "It's all so beautiful!"

"Here's my closet . . ." Chelsea wanted Kesha to find the right clothes for tomorrow and then get out before anyone knew she was there.

Kesha finally looked over all the clothes in the closet. "You have enough here for five girls!"

Chelsea flushed. She did have a lot of clothes. "Do I have anything that'll look right for tomorrow?"

"I don't know." Kesha pushed aside a few items. "Hey, here's something!" She pulled out a bold purple top and shorts and tossed them on the bed. Next she lifted out a pink shirt and a multicolored vest. She tossed them on the bed, then turned to Chelsea. "You got any tights?"

"Sure." Chelsea opened a drawer and showed her neatly folded tights.

"Wow!" Kesha shook her head. "I've got three pairs, but you've got almost a whole drawer full!" She looked through them and finally pulled out the hot pink ones. "Perfect. Just perfect. Now try everything on."

Chelsea pulled off her slacks and top and slipped on the hot pink tights with the purple shorts over them. She put on her purple top, then the pink shirt and the vest.

"Now for your hair . . ." Kesha sat Chelsea on the chair, pulled her hair up high, and put a wide pink band around it. She let go, and the long ponytail flopped down almost over Chelsea's left eye. "Perfect. Just perfect. Now look in the mirror."

Chelsea closed her eyes, took a deep breath, and stepped in front of her mirror. Was that really Chelsea Leighann McCrea? She looked like a girl on TV advertising gum or a soft drink. "I don't know if I can wear this to school."

"You look just like I want you to look!" Kesha laughed and nodded. "*Nobody* will miss you now!"

Chelsea said in a tiny voice, "My mom won't let me wear this. She'll make me change."

"Oh, that's no problem. Wear your regular stuff, then after she sees you, run upstairs, change, and slip out the door before she sees you again."

"I don't know if I can do that." Chelsea's chest felt as if a tight belt circled it. She'd never ever done such a sneaky thing! "I just don't know."

"You can do it. It's easy." Kesha looked in the mirror again. "I'm really pretty, don't you think?"

Chelsea nodded.

"I wonder if others think so." Kesha turned

quickly away. "Why worry about what others think? I'm out to make myself happy. That's what counts. Right, Chel Sea?"

"Right," Chelsea whispered. But was Kesha really right?

Several minutes later, dressed in jeans and a blue T-shirt, Chelsea tried to rush Kesha to the door, but Kesha kept stopping to look at things. Chelsea opened the door. Warm September air rushed in. "See you tomorrow."

Kesha nodded.

"How are you getting home?"

Kesha shrugged. "I'll walk."

"Where do you live?"

"Close to downtown."

"That's a long walk!"

"So? I can do it. I walk a lot." Kesha laughed as she sauntered out the door. She turned at the end of the sidewalk and waved.

Chelsea lifted her hand, then slowly closed the door and weakly leaned against it. Tomorrow school wouldn't be so frightening. Or would it?

Just then someone knocked on the front door. Chelsea jumped. Had Kesha come back? Chelsea hesitated, then opened the door. Hannah and Roxie stood there.

"Kathy will be here soon," Roxie said. "Wasn't school the best today?"

Before Chelsea could answer, Kathy called from

the driveway. She dropped her bike and ran across the lawn.

"She's sure excited about something," Hannah said.

Chelsea watched Kathy's blonde curls bob as she ran up the steps. Chelsea closed the door and started down the steps. The Best Friends knew they couldn't go inside if either her mom or dad wasn't there.

"Let's go to the picnic table," Roxie said, leading the way to the back of the house. Gracie barked, and Roxie frowned. "We got a note from Grandma. She and Ezra are enjoying all the sights of Hawaii on their honeymoon."

"You'll get used to them being married." Hannah brushed a leaf off the bench and sat down. "I keep telling you Ezra's not as grouchy as you think."

"I know . . . I know." Roxie sat on the picnic table and rested her feet on the bench. "I decided I might play tennis this year. What do you think?"

Chelsea shrugged as she and Kathy sat on the table beside Roxie. It was hard for Chelsea to keep her mind on what the others were saying. She kept thinking about Kesha. Chelsea thought about telling the girls all about Kesha, but Kathy started talking about cheerleading.

"The tryouts are next week." Kathy's face glowed, and her hazel eyes sparkled. She brushed back her blonde curls, but they sprang right back. "I'm going to get a red skirt and a red-and-white top to wear since those are the school colors. I'll even wear red socks and white sneakers."

"You'll do great." Hannah nodded and smiled. "I watched you practice, and I was really impressed."

Laughing breathlessly, Roxie leaped to the ground and faced the girls. "I have the very best news in the entire world!"

"What?" Kathy asked at the same time Hannah did. They looked at each other and giggled.

Chelsea tried to feel excited but couldn't.

Roxie looped her thumbs in the pockets of her jeans. "Mrs. Evans, the principal, asked if I'd bring in my carvings so they could display them in the display case in the hall near the front door. My carvings!"

Chelsea heard the others cry out in delight, but she managed only a whispered, "That's great."

"I have the mouse, of course." Roxie rolled her eyes. "I carved that last year. And the squirrel and raccoon. I'm almost finished with a dog . . . one that does not look like Gracie!" She motioned to the small brown dog tied at the base of the deck. "So I'll take them in for the entire middle school to see! She wants them left until after Parents' Day next month!"

Kathy lifted her chin and squared her shoulders. "We'll all walk around and say we're best friends with the great artist Roxann Shoulders. It'll make us practically as famous as you."

Hannah giggled. "I don't think it works that way. Otherwise you'd be famous already because your dad is a TV celebrity."

"Not quite a celebrity. He's the head musician on a TV talk show. He does get fan mail though. Brody and Duke like to read it. Brody wants to be a lead guitar player in a Christian band some day."

"He's good enough, Kathy." Roxie jumped back up on the table. "I love listening to him."

"So do I." Kathy nodded. "I'm sure glad he's my foster brother. He and Duke and I have a lot of fun together."

Chelsea's mind drifted to Kesha as the girls chattered on and on about school and home and family.

Just then Mike ran to Gracie and untied her. "I'm taking her for a walk, Chelsea. I'll be back soon."

Chelsea nodded. Mike acted like taking care of Gracie for Ezra was the most important job in the universe. "Make sure you stay on this block, Mike," she called after him.

"I know that already," he shouted back as Gracie tugged him forward at a run.

Hannah laughed. "He's so cute. I can't wait until baby Burke is that old. All he can do is eat and sleep and smile a little."

"That's what babies do." Roxie hugged her knees. "I remember when Faye was born. I wanted to play with her, but she slept most of the time." Roxie rolled her eyes. "Now I wish she'd sleep when she wants me to play with her."

"How does she like preschool?" Hannah asked.

"She loves it! She'd go all the time if Mom would let her."

"Wait'll she starts real school," Chelsea said. "She'll change her mind."

"That's for sure!" Kathy nodded. "I remember when I was in kindergarten, I liked the toys and the kids. Except for Roy Marks. He kept pulling my hair and taking my toys."

Roxie frowned thoughtfully. "Roy Marks. I saw him today."

Kathy flushed. "I did too. Doesn't he have the bluest eyes in the entire world?"

Roxie and Hannah giggled and jabbed Kathy. Chelsea looked off across the lawn. She heard the girls, but it was like they were in a different dimension.

"Would you go with him if he asked you?" Roxie asked.

Kathy frowned. "I'm not allowed to go out with a boy."

"Would you eat lunch with him and stuff like that?"

Kathy ducked her head and grinned. "Well . . . maybe."

"Chel, did you see Clay Ross today?" Roxie asked.

At the sound of her name Chelsea pulled her mind back. "Clay Ross?"

"You know . . ." Kathy tugged Chelsea's hair. ". . . the boy you liked for a while. Remember?"

Chelsea's face turned as red as her hair. She'd liked Clay Ross so much that she'd ruined Roxie's chance at winning the art contest this summer. "What about him?"

"Did you see him today?"

"No."

"He's in seventh grade." Hannah patted Chelsea. "That's why you didn't see him."

"Probably." Chelsea moved restlessly. It was hard to sit still and listen to the girls. She'd never felt that way since they'd all four become best friends. Things were sure different now that school had started.

"Did you get the Scripture for today, Chel?" Kathy asked.

Chelsea frowned. "Me? Was I supposed to have it?"

"You said you would. Is something wrong?" Kathy looked closely at Chelsea.

"It's her first day at a new school," Hannah said quickly. "I can see why she'd forget things."

"I have a Scripture," Roxie said. "It's only part of Galatians 5:13. 'Serve one another in love.'" Roxie smiled. "That's what we're supposed to do . . . serve each other and others around us in love, don't have a fit about helping."

Chelsea thought about Kesha and her help. Once again Chelsea started to tell the Best Friends about Kesha. But just as she opened her mouth Hannah jumped up.

"I've got to get home. See you all tomorrow!"

Chelsea watched as they all left, leaving her standing in her yard alone. Slowly she walked toward the house. How could she face tomorrow? "Kesha will help me," she whispered.

She sighed heavily as she slipped inside the silent house.

3

Chelsea's New Look

Chelsea almost choked on a bite of toast as Mom set a plate of scrambled eggs on the table. Chelsea moved restlessly. Could she really slip back upstairs and change into the clothes Kesha had chosen for her? Under her jeans she already wore her pink tights. She was wearing the purple top. She only had to put on the pink shirt and the multicolored vest, then fix her hair.

Mom sat at the table and looked at Chelsea, Mike, and Rob. "I have wonderful news. I planned to tell you last night, but things got a little hectic."

Chelsea flushed. The "hectic" stuff Mom was talking about was the fight she and Rob had had over who was going to do the dishes. Chelsea had been sure it was Rob's turn, but he finally proved it was hers. They almost never fought over anything like most brothers and sisters did.

"What's the news?" Rob asked.

"I finally got the hours at work I want—from

8:30 to 3:00. So I'll be here every day when you get home after school. Starting today." She smiled happily.

Chelsea's heart dropped to her feet. How could she get in the house without Mom seeing what she was wearing?

"That's great, Mom!" Rob said.

"But don't take Gracie for a walk." Mike looked worried. "I want to when I get home."

Mom laughed. "Don't worry, Mike. I wouldn't think of taking the dog for a walk."

Chelsea excused herself, put her dirty plate, glass, and fork in the dishwasher, then ran upstairs. Things had really changed. She could almost hear Kesha say, "Find a way to do what you want . . . That's what's important."

Chelsea spotted her book bag. She could put her shorts in the bag and change in the school restroom. Trembling, she rolled up her shorts and stuck them in her pack. Quickly she changed from her jeans to her skirt. She pulled on the blouse and the vest. She'd fix her hair on the bus. She darted a look in the mirror and groaned. This was definitely not the real Chelsea McCrea. She made a face. Nobody ever noticed the real Chelsea, so she'd become someone they would notice!

She slipped downstairs and opened the front door. "I'm going, Mom." She closed the door quickly before Mom could answer—or even tell her to come back for the Scripture for the day or to wait for Mike and Rob.

The September breeze blew against Chelsea. She saw Hannah leave her yard and look toward her house. Chelsea ducked behind a tree so Hannah wouldn't see her. Hannah would try to talk her out of her new look.

Finally Chelsea reached the bus stop. Hannah was busy with her sisters, and Roxie was talking to a couple of girls. Chelsea ducked behind two tall high school boys so her friends couldn't see her. She slipped into the bus and sat close to the front with the same two girls as yesterday. As soon as the bus pulled away from the curb, Chelsea pulled her hair to the top of her head and put the band in place. The ponytail flipped down over her eyes. She pushed it back, and it flipped right back. Impatiently she pulled out the band, pulled her hair further back, and twisted the band in place again. This time her ponytail flipped just where she wanted it. She tied the ribbon in place and then folded her hands in her lap.

The two little girls looked at Chelsea, then smiled. "You're beautiful!" they said together.

"Thanks." She ducked her head. Her ponytail slipped over her forehead.

"I wish I could look just like you," the girl nearest her said.

"What's your name?" asked the other.

"Chelsea."

"I like that name. I'm Susan, and this is Abby. We're in first grade. What grade are you in?"

"Sixth." Smiling, Chelsea settled back and talked

with the girls all the way to school. Her new look did indeed make a difference!

At the middle school Chelsea walked off the bus with her head high. "Hi," she said to a girl standing off to one side of the sidewalk.

The girl's eyes widened, but she smiled and said, "Hi."

Chelsea walked toward the school. She smiled and said hi to several students. Most of them greeted her in return. When she was almost at the door of the school she spotted Hannah, Roxie, and Kathy. They were looking at her in shock. She flushed, then turned her head and waved at someone.

Roxie ran over to Chelsea and eyed her up and down. "Is that you, Chelsea?"

"Sure is!" Chelsea's nerves tightened, but she kept a wide smile on her face. "Isn't it a beautiful day?"

Hannah and Kathy stared at Chelsea. "We never saw you like this before," Kathy said.

"I'm totally made over!" Chelsea flipped the hem of her vest. "I like the clothes, don't you?"

"They're really bright," Hannah said. She smiled and nodded. "You look like a picture in a teen magazine."

"Thanks." Just then Chelsea spotted Kesha. She was wearing the same clothes as yesterday. Chelsea smiled at Hannah. "Gotta go." She ran away from the Best Friends and walked into the school with Kesha beside her. Chelsea glanced over her shoulder and saw the Best Friends staring after her. Her heart turned over, but she forced a laugh.

"You're sure not invisible now," Kesha said as they started up the crowded stairs.

"I talked to more people in the last few minutes than I did all day yesterday. It's great!"

"Who were the girls you were talking to just before you ran over to me?"

Chelsea hesitated, then shrugged. "Just some girls I met this summer." She felt sad about her own words, but she couldn't take them back.

"Well, don't hang around them or you'll end up looking and acting like you did yesterday. You stay with me and this will be your best school year yet." Kesha shoved past a boy and almost knocked over a girl. "Hurry, Chel Sea, or we won't get our choice of seats."

Chelsea frowned slightly but followed Kesha into their homeroom. Kesha stood just inside the room and looked all around. There were already several students there, talking and laughing. Finally Kesha walked to the front row. Only one chair was empty. Kesha motioned for Chelsea to sit there. Her legs trembling, Chelsea sat down. She groaned. The front row! Could she really handle everyone staring at her?

Kesha leaned down to the girl sitting on the seat next to Chelsea. "I need to sit here. Would you mind moving?"

The girl shrugged. "I was here first."

"So? You could sit just behind."

"You could too."

Chelsea jumped up. "I'll sit back there, and you sit here, Kesha."

But Kesha just shook her head and looked very stubborn. She bumped the girl's legs. "Go back there or I'll embarrass you in front of the whole room."

The girl hesitated, then slipped out of her chair and into the second row. Kesha sat down, a look of triumph on her face. She leaned over to Chelsea. "That's how to do it."

Chelsea bit her lip. She didn't know if she wanted to be so pushy.

Mr. Borgman walked up to his desk and looked at the students. Today he wore a tan jacket over dark pants and a white shirt with a flowered tie.

Kesha raised her hand and before he even called on her said, "Mr. Borgman, I'm Kesha Bronski, and this is Chel Sea McCrea. If you want us to read aloud, we will."

"Thank you." Mr. Borgman smiled at Kesha and then at Chelsea.

Chelsea sat very still. Would he say anything about her strange clothes? He didn't, and she was relieved.

In math class Kesha dragged Chelsea up to Mrs. Williams. The teacher sat behind her desk with her glasses in her hand. She was about thirty years old with short brown hair and wide brown eyes. "Hi, Mrs. Williams. I'm Kesha, and this is Chel Sea. We'd like to sit together please. We're both new in school."

Mrs. William looked at her seating chart, then up at Kesha. "Sorry, girls. We have assigned seats. You're already here and here." She tapped the spots with the eraser on her yellow pencil.

"Will you make an exception for us?" Kesha leaned down to Mrs. Williams. "I really should've told you yesterday. Sometimes Chel Sea has trouble with . . . well, you know . . . and she needs me to give her a hand getting to the restroom."

Chelsea wanted to sink through the floor as Mrs. Williams studied her intently.

"I don't have a note about any special condition," Mrs. Williams said softly. She fingered the white beads that hung down her bright blue blouse, then touched her round white earrings.

"Because she doesn't want to be embarrassed," Kesha whispered. "We could sit right up here near the front. We won't cause a bit of trouble. Honest. Will we, Chel Sea?"

Her face flaming, Chelsea shook her head.

Mrs. Williams patted Chelsea's hand. "If you have any difficulty at all, dear, let me know."

"Thank you," Chelsea whispered.

"Mrs. Williams, if you need help with anything, let us know," Kesha said.

"Thank you." Mrs. Williams looked at her chart, erased a couple of names, and wrote in Chelsea's and Kesha's. "Sit right there. I'll let the other girls know of the change."

"I knew you'd understand." Kesha smiled, then jabbed Chelsea.

She managed to smile, then sank to her seat, her legs weak. What else would Kesha say or do? Chelsea glanced at her new friend and saw that she was writing frantically on a piece of paper. When she finished she thrust it at Chelsea.

"What is it?"

"Answers to a quiz she's going to give us," Kesha whispered.

Chelsea frowned.

"I saw the quiz on her desk and memorized the answers."

"That's impossible!"

Kesha shrugged. "Not to me."

Chelsea wanted to crumple up the paper, but she didn't. Kesha was probably making it up.

Mrs. Williams called the class to order, took roll, then said, "I'd like all of you to meet two new students. They're right here in the front row looking like two lovely, bright birds . . . Kesha Bronski and Chelsea McCrea. Girls, stand up and greet the others."

Kesha jumped right up, turned and waved, and said, "Hi!"

Chelsea slowly stood, even more slowly turned to face the others, then whispered, "Hi." She saw the surprise on the Best Friends' faces. With a low moan she sank back into her seat.

Mrs. Williams walked to the corner of her desk

and leaned against it. "I'm going to give you a short quiz today so I can see just where we are in math."

Everyone groaned. Chelsea shot a startled look at Kesha, who looked very smug.

"Take out a paper and write these problems down." Mrs. Williams dictated the problems one at a time. "You have ten minutes." She sat down and folded her hands on her desk.

Kesha finished the problems in a couple of minutes. She waved her hand high. "I'm finished. Shall I bring my paper to you?"

"You can't be done already."

"I'm very good in math."

Mrs. Williams looked skeptical. "Bring your paper here and let me see."

Chelsea's stomach cramped painfully. She would not cheat, no matter what! She watched Mrs. Williams slip on her glasses and quickly look over Kesha's paper.

"They're all correct! Kesha, I'm astonished."

Kesha flashed a smile at whoever was looking and sat back down.

Chelsea struggled with the problems and finally finished. She handed in her paper and had one wrong. She didn't care. It was better than cheating.

While Mrs. Williams talked with a few students at her desk, Kesha leaned over to Chelsea. "Why didn't you use the answers I gave you?"

Chelsea shook her head. "I couldn't . . . Cheating is wrong."

Kesha frowned. "Baloney! As long as you know

how to do the math, what does it matter if you copy the answers?"

Chelsea shrugged. She couldn't talk about it now. She didn't want anyone to overhear and think she'd planned to cheat. She'd never cheated in her life, and not even Kesha would make her.

Suddenly Kesha jumped up and hauled Chelsea up with her. "Mrs. Williams, may we be excused? It's urgent!"

"Yes!" Mrs. Williams looked worried. "Do you need help?"

"No. I can manage. Hurry, Chel Sea!" Kesha pushed Chelsea ahead of her toward the door.

Chelsea glanced at the students, and her eyes locked with Hannah's. Chelsea flushed, and Hannah looked concerned.

"Hurry up!" Kesha pushed Chelsea harder, and she almost fell through the door.

In the hall Kesha covered her mouth and laughed. "We got out of there, didn't we? Now we can spend the rest of the hour in the restroom."

Her heart sinking, Chelsea slowly walked along behind Kesha.

4

The Long Hour

In the restroom Chelsea turned to Kesha. She was fixing the lime-green clip in her curly blonde ponytail. "Why did you want out of math class?"

Kesha shrugged. She patted her lime-green shorts and lifted a strand of hair off her bold orange tights. "It's boring. Why stay there? I've got better things to do. And you should feel the same." Kesha giggled and flipped her ponytail. "We do look like two bright birds. I wish I had red hair like yours! Hey, maybe I should dye it!" She headed for the door. "Let's go buy some dye right now."

Chelsea ran after Kesha and caught her arm. "We can't leave school to go shopping!"

Chuckling, Kesha pulled free. "I've done it a lot."

"Please . . ." Chelsea struggled to hold back the tears. "I don't want to."

"Oh, all right! Let's go look around then. I read on the bulletin board that the eighth graders were having a special photography meeting with Mr. Scott. You like photography?"

"Yes! I want to learn how to take better photographs. But how can we even get in? We're sixth graders."

"So we fake it."

Chelsea blew out her breath. "I've never done anything like that."

"I can tell." Kesha giggled. "You've always been the little girl who obeys and leads a very boring life."

"Not boring exactly."

"Let's go look." Kesha pushed open the restroom door and stepped out into the empty hallway.

Chelsea locked her fingers together and looked longingly toward the classroom she should've been in. Lockers lined both walls between doorways. "I want to go back to math class."

"Fine," Kesha snapped. "Go! I'll be all right on my own."

Chelsea sighed heavily. "Oh, all right, I'll go with you." She looked up and down the hall. Scuff marks marred the tiled floor. The ceiling lights seemed too bright and too revealing. Smells of coffee and cigarette smoke drifted out from the teachers' lounge.

With her head high Kesha walked down the hall, her orange and lime colors even brighter than the ceiling lights. Finally Chelsea hurried after her. Just as they were walking past the library a teacher Chelsea didn't know hurried out. She had gray hair and wore a black suit and a flowered blouse. She frowned at Kesha and Chelsea.

"Do you girls have a pass to be in the hall?"

Chelsea's body pricked with nervous heat.

Kesha smiled and stepped closer to Chelsea. "We're on our way to the restroom. Mrs. Williams asked if I'd go with Chelsea since she was ... well, you know ... having a problem."

"The restroom nearest your class is back that way."

"Oh! Thank you! We're both new. We didn't know."

Chelsea's heart sank. Another lie!

Kesha caught Chelsea's arm. "Hurry, Chel Sea! I told you we could be going the wrong way! Hold on a little longer." Kesha gripped Chelsea's arm and rushed back the way they'd come.

Chelsea felt hot, then cold, then hot again. All she wanted to do was go back to math and finish out the hour.

At the restroom door Kesha glanced back. "She's gone ... Let's go back!"

"Please, Kesha, let's go to math class instead."

Kesha wagged her finger in Chelsea's face. "You go back if you want, but I'm going to photography class." Kesha waited. "Well, make up your mind—are you coming with me or not?"

Chelsea sighed heavily. She really didn't have the courage to go back to class alone. Everybody would notice her, especially dressed the way she was. "I'll go with you."

"I thought so!" Kesha giggled, and her brown eyes glowed. "You and me both like lots of excitement."

Chelsea groaned. She liked excitement, but not nearly as much as Kesha did.

Suddenly Kesha stopped. "Look! An open locker!"

"Don't!" Chelsea darted a look around, but no one was in sight.

"I like looking at others' things, don't you?" Kesha peered inside the locker. "It's a boy's." She touched a blue jacket and picked up a baseball mitt. A pack of gum lay on the shelf, and she started to take a piece but then put it back.

"Please, Kesha, let's go," Chelsea whispered, trembling as she looked around again.

Kesha giggled and partly closed the locker door so it was exactly the way she'd found it. "He'll never know anyone looked through his stuff or touched his gum." She flipped her ponytail and walked on, her sneakers quiet on the floor.

Chelsea looked longingly over her shoulder. She could run back to class and leave Kesha on her own. Chelsea bit her lip. She couldn't face walking into the classroom all alone.

Kesha ran down the flight of stairs and stopped outside the boys' restroom. "I've always wondered if it looks the same as ours."

Chelsea gasped. "Don't you dare go in there! What if a boy's in there?"

Kesha giggled and nudged Chelsea in the arm. "I'm only teasing. I'd never look in the boys' restroom." She hurried on down the hall and stopped outside a closed door marked "Teachers' Lounge." "But I do want to look in here."

"No!" Chelsea shook her head so hard, her ponytail danced wildly.

Kesha pressed her ear to the door. "Sounds empty," she whispered. She knocked, waited, then knocked again.

Chelsea's knees knocked harder than Kesha's fist on the door.

Grinning, Kesha opened the door and looked inside. "Empty . . . Come on!" She jerked Chelsea into the room and closed the door.

Chelsea nervously looked around. A big table with chairs pushed up to it stood to one side of the room. Two blue plaid sofas were pushed against a wall. A tall pot of coffee and a box of sweet rolls sat on a counter beside a sink and a microwave oven.

Kesha opened the box of rolls, broke off a piece, and ate it. "Ummm—delicious. Want a bite?" She held a piece toward Chelsea.

"No . . . No." Chelsea's stomach knotted, and she reached to open the door. "Let's get out of here right now!"

"You're not only bright-colored like a bird—you scare as easily as one." Kesha giggled as she got a drink of water in a paper cup. She tossed the cup into the wastebasket. "Sure you don't want a roll?"

"No!"

Kesha shrugged, opened the door, stepped out— and almost ran into a tall man wearing a gray suit.

Chelsea wanted to duck back inside the room and hide behind the sofa. But she stood silently beside Kesha and stared up at the man as he frowned down at them.

"The teachers' lounge is off-limits to students," the man said sharply.

"We know." Kesha smiled. "We were looking for Chel Sea's mom. A teacher asked her to meet her in there."

Chelsea bit back a sharp cry.

"She's not there," Kesha said, looking worried. "Where do you think we should look next? She said a teachers' lounge . . . Maybe she meant on the second floor."

The man nodded. "Could be. Run on and see." He walked on without a backward look.

Chelsea covered her face and moaned.

Kesha jabbed Chelsea. "Hey, we didn't get caught, did we? We're doing okay, so quit worrying."

"Can't we just go back to class now?"

"Nope!" Kesha led the way to a corner room with "Photography" marked on the door. She smiled at Chelsea.

"Don't go in," Chelsea whispered.

Kesha grinned, opened the door, slipped inside,

and jerked Chelsea in with her. Students stood at the front of the room listening to the instructor talk about focusing a camera and watching him work. Color and black-and-white photographs covered a huge bulletin board; a special light shone down on it. A table stood in the back of the room with a still-life arrangement on it.

The instructor wore jeans and a loose shirt. He had light brown hair that reached his shoulders. He glanced at Kesha and Chelsea. "May I help you girls?"

Kesha stepped forward with a wide smile. "Mr. Scott, we're sorry to be late, but Mrs. Evans said to come anyway."

Chelsea froze. Mrs. Evans was the principal, and she'd never said anything of the kind.

"Do you have a pass?" The instructor held out his hand.

Kesha turned to Chelsea. "Give it to him, Chel Sea." She turned back to the instructor. "I'm Kesha Bronski. My family just moved here from St. Paul. This is Chel Sea McCrea from Oklahoma. She's never lived in Michigan before. Just tell us what we're supposed to do and we'll do it." Kesha peered at the camera. "Is that a Nikon N2000 with a A1-S Nikkor Lens? I used that in St. Paul for my last project." She turned to Chelsea. "Didn't you tell me you had too?"

Chelsea shrugged helplessly. Kesha made up too many stories for Chelsea to keep up with.

"Okay, girls. Let me get back to talking about

how to focus in this light." Mr. Scott continued talking.

Chelsea wanted to rush from the room, but Kesha held her arm. Kesha chuckled under her breath.

Mr. Scott set the camera down and walked to the photographs on the wall. He pointed to a shadowed photo of an old barn with a windmill beside it.

Chelsea studied the picture. It reminded her of Oklahoma. She listened intently as Mr. Scott explained why he'd decided to take that angle for the shot and how he'd set up to do it. She understood what he said and knew she could remember to do it the next time she was taking pictures.

Just as Mr. Scott was giving an assignment for the next day, Kesha dragged Chelsea out of the room and down the hall to the stairs. "So what did you think, Chel Sea?"

"It was great!" Chelsea's eyes sparkled. "I want to join that class!"

Kesha frowned. "You can't *join*. You can only sneak in once in a while."

"But there has to be a way for me to get into the class and learn more about photography."

"There is a Photography Club you can join."

"Then let's join!"

Kesha frowned. "It's after school every Wednesday."

"So?"

Kesha shrugged.

"We'll join. It'll be great. Then we won't have to sneak into Mr. Scott's class."

Kesha slowly started up the stairs. "Right now we have to get to science class."

Chelsea groaned. Would the Best Friends ask her why she hadn't returned to math class? If so, what would she say? Could she tell them the truth? Shivers ran down her spine.

Just then she remembered that Mrs. Williams was not only their math teacher, but their science teacher too. Chelsea stopped short at the top of the stairs. "What'll we do? Mrs. Williams will ask where we were all hour."

"So what's to tell? We stayed in the restroom until you could manage to leave it." Kesha grinned and shrugged. "We won't wait until she asks us—we'll go right up to her and explain. It'll work. You'll see."

Helplessly Chelsea shook her head and walked behind Kesha into science.

5

The Longest Day

Chelsea sank into the seat she'd been assigned yesterday in science. Kesha sat beside her. "That's not your seat," Chelsea whispered.

"So?"

Chelsea touched her hot cheek. "Please, Kesha, I can't do this all day long!"

"Do what?"

"Be so . . . *different!*"

Kesha giggled. "You're funny."

Hannah stopped beside Chelsea, glanced quickly at Kesha, then bent down to Chelsea and whispered, "Are you all right?"

Burning with embarrassment, Chelsea nodded. She longed to have Hannah sit beside her, but she knew Hannah wouldn't. She already had an assigned seat.

"Kathy and Roxie are worried too."

"They are?"

Kesha jabbed Chelsea in the arm. "We've got to talk to Mrs. Williams."

"Oh, okay. See ya later, Hannah." Chelsea longingly watched Hannah return to her seat.

Kesha laughed. "Hannah? I thought you didn't know her. She's an American Indian, isn't she?"

"Ottawa."

"She should wear a headband and fringed leather jacket."

"I'll tell her."

Kesha frowned at Chelsea. "Do you know her well enough to tell her that?"

Chelsea hunched her shoulders. "I guess."

"Then why isn't she helping you get used to the new school?" Kesha shrugged. "Never mind . . . Come on."

Hesitantly Chelsea walked with Kesha to talk to Mrs. Williams.

"Sorry we couldn't get back to math class, Mrs. Williams," Kesha said in a low voice. "Chel Sea seems okay now."

Mrs. Williams smiled. "Good."

"I need to sit with her in this class too."

With a quick erase and a write-in Mrs. Williams switched Kesha with the boy who had sat beside Chelsea yesterday.

Her two tops and vest feeling suddenly very hot, Chelsea walked back to her seat and sank down. The eyes of every student in the room seemed to be boring holes right through her.

Kesha plopped down in her newly assigned seat. "See? It worked."

Chelsea helplessly shook her head. The band around her ponytail felt too tight. The hum of voices around her seemed miles away. In a daze she heard Mrs. Williams take roll and begin the class. She automatically opened her science book to the page Mrs. Williams announced to the class. The chapter began with a study of clouds. Chelsea yawned with boredom. She peeked sideways at Kesha, expecting her to be bored too, but she was listening with interest. She even asked an intelligent question, then later answered a question Mrs. Williams asked.

Chelsea glanced back at Hannah. She had her head down and looked sad. Chelsea wished she could write a note and send it back to her, but she didn't dare. She'd make sure to eat lunch with Hannah today and ask what was wrong. Somehow they'd missed each other at lunch period the day before, but today . . .

After science Chelsea tried to wait for Hannah to tell her to meet her for lunch, but Kesha hurried her down the crowded hall to computer class. Chelsea had tried to get out of taking computer class, but it was required.

"I hate this class," Chelsea whispered.

Kesha giggled. "Leave it to me." She marched right up to Mr. Lincoln. She whispered to him and pointed back at Chelsea.

Chelsea burned with embarrassment. She ducked

her head and tried to look invisible. *Invisible?* That's what she hadn't wanted to be yesterday.

Soon Kesha hurried over to her and put her arm around her. "Lean on me and look sick," she whispered.

Chelsea didn't have to pretend. She *was* sick! Would this terrible day ever end?

Kesha walked Chelsea to the end of the hall, glanced back, then ducked around the corner. "I said you were sick and that I was taking you to the restroom and maybe even the school nurse."

"Kesha, I wish you wouldn't lie."

"Lie?" Kesha looked deeply hurt. "I'm not lying—I'm only making up stories to get us out of class."

"It's *lying*, Kesha."

She shook her head and looked upset for a short while and then giggled. "We got out of computer class, didn't we? That's all that counts. What shall we do now? Go buy red dye?"

"Kesha!"

"Oh, all right!" Kesha ran to an exit door and peered through the glass. "It looks sunny and nice out. Come on!"

Chelsea groaned, but she followed Kesha outside. The warm wind felt good against Chelsea's burning skin. She looked across the wide, grassy, tree-shaded yard and over at the bus garage, then on to two homes circled by white picket fences.

Kesha breathed deeply and spread her arms wide.

"When I grow up and have a house of my own, I want a gigantic yard."

"A yard is nice, but it takes a lot of work."

"Work?"

"Sure. Mowing and raking . . . trimming bushes . . . planting flowers. I love doing flowers!"

Kesha's eyes widened in surprise. "Don't you have someone do that work for you?"

"No. Do you?"

Kesha laughed. "I don't even have a yard or flowers!"

"Oh."

Kesha caught Chelsea's hand, dashed to a tree, and slipped around it out of sight of the school windows. They sat in the soft grass and leaned back against the rough bark of the tree.

"When I come to your house next, can I work in the yard with you, Chel Sea?"

"Sure . . . I guess so." Chelsea couldn't imagine Kesha wanting to work in the yard.

"Do you ever wish you could trade places with someone?"

Chelsea shrugged. "Do you?"

"Of course!"

Chelsea turned her head so she could see Kesha. "Who would you trade places with?"

Kesha sighed deeply. "With anyone who lived in one place all the time. Someone with a big house, a yard, a mom who talked to me, even baked cookies with me. And a dad who smiled at me a lot and called me a pet name. Does your dad call you a pet name?"

Chelsea flushed and giggled. "Hon bun."

Kesha giggled. "Hon bun?"

"Yeah. It's dumb, isn't it?"

Kesha wiped a tear off her lashes. "Real dumb."

Chelsea pulled her knees to her chin as they talked. The hour slipped quickly away. Then they ran back inside the school without anyone seeing them. Chelsea caught sight of Mrs. Williams. Shivers ran up and down her spine.

At lunch Kesha dragged Chelsea toward the cafeteria before she had a chance to find Hannah. At the door Chelsea grabbed the doorjamb and held on to it.

"Wait, Kesha!"

"Why?"

"For Hannah."

Kesha looked over the crowd. "I don't see her. Do you?"

Chelsea looked around and shook her head.

"We can catch her inside."

"Okay." Chelsea walked through the line. She took one piece of pizza and a can of apple juice. Her stomach lurched, and she wondered if she could even eat that much. She watched Kesha fill her tray.

Kesha led Chelsea to an empty table, and they sat side by side and ate in silence. Kesha ate everything on her tray. Chelsea left part of her pizza and half her juice.

"Can I have the rest of your pizza?"

"Sure."

Kesha ate the piece in a few bites. "School food's not that good, is it?"

Chelsea shrugged. She strained her neck to look all around the room. She couldn't see the Best Friends anywhere. Hadn't they eaten today?

"Who are you looking for?"

"Hannah."

"Oh, she'll turn up. Let's go. Maybe we can get that red dye."

Chelsea emptied her tray and hurried out of the noisy cafeteria with Kesha. "I won't leave the school. I mean it, Kesha!"

Kesha stopped in the hallway with her hands on her hips. "Can't you ever just have fun?"

"I can have fun, but I won't break the rules by leaving the school."

Kesha stepped right up to Chelsea. "I didn't plan to leave school. I can get the dye afterward. But I want to do something really exciting. Let's go to English class early and see if we can do something in there."

Still looking for the Best Friends, Chelsea hurried along with Kesha.

A tall, dark-haired girl stopped them near the English room. "I just love your clothes," she said with a sneer.

"Thanks." Kesha struck a model's pose and turned slowly. "You'd look this good if you dressed this way."

Chelsea forced a smile. Maybe Kesha didn't know the girl was making fun of them.

The girl snickered and walked away. She stopped and called over her shoulder, "Go live in the zoo where you belong!"

Kesha knotted her fists and shouted, "You're just jealous!"

The girl spun around and glared at them. "You're both too dumb to know how ugly you look!"

Chelsea trembled.

"We aren't invisible like you are!" Kesha cried.

Chelsea shook Kesha's arm. "Shhh! The teachers will hear and send us to the office."

"So? I've been sent to the principal's office in every school I've been to."

Chelsea tugged on Kesha. "Come on! We're going to English class, remember?"

Kesha turned away from the girl and walked through the door with Chelsea. Kesha brushed at her eyes.

Chelsea looked at her closely. Was Kesha crying? The room was empty. Chelsea sank to a seat and took a deep breath. She felt as if she'd gone through a whole month in just a half a day.

Kesha sat down and took a deep breath.

"You okay?"

Kesha shrugged.

"I'm sorry she made fun of you."

"And you!"

"I know. Maybe we are too . . . too bright."

"Too bad! I'll dress however I want." Kesha jumped up with a laugh. "Chel Sea, let's change clothes. You wear my stuff, and I'll wear yours!"

"Why?"

"Just to be different."

"Want me to bring something tomorrow for you?"

Kesha nodded. "Wait! I'll ride home with you again today! I can get something from your closet to wear tomorrow."

Chelsea didn't know if Mom would allow that. "I have to ask my mom."

"Why would she care?"

"I don't know. I just have to ask her."

"She wouldn't even have to know."

Chelsea swallowed hard. "She's going to be home when I get there. She'd know."

"Oh." Kesha sank to a desk. "Does she wait at the door for you?"

"Sometimes."

"Does she bake cookies?"

"Sometimes."

"I saw a mom on TV like that."

"What about your mom?"

Kesha laughed gruffly. "Who knows?"

Chelsea wanted to ask more, but just then several students walked in and sat down.

Kesha smiled brightly at them. "Hi. I'm Kesha, and this is Chel Sea. We're new."

"Hi," a blonde girl said with a smile. "I'm Brenda. I like your clothes."

"Thanks." Kesha spun around with her arms out.

"I'd like to wear shorts to school, but my mom won't let me," a short, dark-haired girl said. "But maybe if I wore tights under them, she would."

"What's your name?" Kesha asked.

"Lucy. And this is Tim, Pete, Laurence, Ruth, Mina, Janice, and Saundra." They all smiled and said hello.

"Have you lived here all your lives?" Chelsea asked.

"Yes," they all said.

"I lived in Oklahoma all my life until this summer."

"Don't you know anyone?" Brenda asked.

"She knows me." Giggling, Kesha spun around again. "And now we know all of you."

Chelsea smiled and relaxed for the first time as they all talked together. She saw the Best Friends walk in, but it was time for the bell, so they took their seats.

During P.E. the girls played softball. Kesha was a good pitcher and let everyone know it. Chelsea felt more herself dressed in her gym shorts and T-shirt. Later she took a shower and slipped on her other clothes. Once again she was a "bright bird."

Just outside the gym Roxie walked over to Chelsea and whispered, "Are you okay?"

Chelsea nodded. But was she really all right?

"See ya at home." Roxie hurried away with a small wave.

Chelsea slowly walked to social studies. Maybe Kesha would sit quietly in this class like she had in English. She did, and Chelsea breathed a sigh of relief.

Finally the bell rang, and the school day was over. Chelsea hurried to her locker and grabbed her book bag. She dashed to the restroom and quickly pulled off her shorts and put on her skirt. She took off her vest and blouse and left on her purple top. She pulled the bow and band from her hair. Quickly she pulled her hair into a normal ponytail and wrapped the band around it. Breathing hard, she raced down the hall and outdoors to the bus. She barely made it into the bus on time.

"Here, Chel Sea!"

She looked up at the sound of Kesha's voice. Kesha sat four rows back and was waving wildly. Chelsea reddened. Slowly she walked back to Kesha and sat down. The bus pulled out with a loud hiss and a lurch.

Kesha tugged on Chelsea's denim skirt. "You changed your clothes!"

"I had to." Chelsea cleared her throat. "Because of my mom."

"Oh . . . Well, you look fine."

"Thanks. I really don't know if I can dress so different tomorrow."

Kesha shrugged. "Then don't. We'll try it your way."

"Really?" Chelsea peered closely at Kesha. What was she up to?

"Sure. You show me what to wear and I'll wear it."

Chelsea locked her hands over her book bag. Could she let Kesha borrow clothes without asking Mom?

6

Kesha

With students swarming and shouting around her, Chelsea hurried ahead of Kesha away from the bus and down the tree-lined sidewalk. Maybe the Best Friends wouldn't know Kesha was with her. None of the Best Friends told lies or cheated or sneaked out of school. *She* didn't even do those things—at least not before she'd met Kesha.

Just then Kesha ran up to Chelsea and slipped her hand through her arm. "This is great! I can't wait to look in your closet again."

"It's just the same."

"Enough clothes for five girls!" Kesha skipped ahead, then turned to walk backwards as she talked to Chelsea. Kesha's brown eyes sparkled, and her cheeks glowed. "If I lived in The Ravines, I'd know *everybody* by now."

After seeing Kesha in action today, Chelsea could easily believe that.

Rob ran past, stopped, and turned around. "Hey, Chelsea . . . hi." He looked uncertainly at Kesha. "Hi."

"Hi. I'm Kesha Bronski." Her white teeth flashed in her brightest smile yet. "Chel Sea's friend."

Rob looked from Chelsea to Kesha and back again.

"I'm going home with her."

"You are?" Rob smiled hesitantly. "I'm Rob McCrea . . . Chelsea's brother."

"You are?" Kesha jabbed Chelsea's arm. "Your brother! How come he talks to you?"

Chelsea frowned. "What do you mean?"

"I've got three brothers, and they hate my guts."

"That's too bad," Chelsea said.

"Chel and I are friends." Rob grinned. "Right, Chel?"

She managed a smile. "Right." And they *were* friends. She just didn't want him hanging around Kesha and learning the truth about what the two of them had been up to.

"Gotta go." Rob dashed down the sidewalk for home.

Kesha sighed enviously. "You have *everything*, don't you?"

As they walked slowly along, Chelsea thought about her life and shook her head. "I still have to go to a strange, new school."

"Oh, that!" Kesha waved her hand. "I've gone to a new school every year of my life."

"How can you stand it?"

Kesha shrugged so hard her head sank between her shoulder blades. "What can I do? I have to go where my dad goes."

"I know!" Chelsea rolled her eyes. She walked more slowly and told Kesha how angry she'd been when Dad had said they were moving to Michigan.

"Are you still mad at him?"

"No. I knew Jesus didn't want me to be."

"Jesus?"

"Yes." Chelsea hesitated. She felt strange talking about Jesus after the way she'd acted today. "Jesus is my friend and my Savior. Is He yours?"

Kesha shrugged. "Never thought about it." She broke into a run. "Race you to the door!"

Chelsea hung back a minute and then ran after Kesha. Just as they reached the door it opened and Mom stood there smiling. She wore faded jeans and a bright green-and-yellow blouse.

"Hello." She kissed Chelsea and then turned to Kesha. "Rob said Chelsea was bringing a friend home. Come in. I'm Billie McCrea."

"I'm Kesha." She laughed gaily. "I'm really glad I got to meet you!"

"Come to the kitchen for a snack. The boys are already there."

Chelsea looked longingly toward the stairs. She wanted to get Kesha in and out before Mom learned anything about the disastrous day. But before she could stop Kesha, she walked into the kitchen, chattering about how much she liked the house, the yard, and even The Ravines. In a minute she might add Chelsea's closet to the list! Chelsea followed them to the kitchen, her heart in her mouth. Mom was smart. She'd pick up on everything Kesha said or even hinted at about their day together.

In the kitchen Chelsea poured herself and Kesha a glass of milk. The boys sat at the table with milk and brownies. Mom rested her hand on Mike's shoulder and smiled.

"Kesha, this is Mike, the youngest in the family."

"And the best," Mike said with a laugh. He had a milk mustache and brownie crumbs on his shirt.

"Do you have brothers and sisters?" Mom asked as she sat down and motioned Kesha to do the same.

Chelsea set a glass of milk in front of Kesha, then sat beside her as Kesha told about her three brothers and two sisters.

"Two brothers are younger than me, and everyone else is older." Kesha sighed. "I don't like being called one of the little kids."

"Or the baby." Mike made a face.

"Somebody has to be the baby." Mom kissed Mike on the head and then turned back to Kesha. "Do your parents both work?"

Chelsea bit into her brownie without tasting it. Would Kesha tell the truth about her family? Or would she make up a story just so it sounded good?

"My dad works wherever he can find a job. Mom mostly stays home and takes care of us kids. She likes to bake cookies and things. She always talks to us and plays games with us and stuff like that."

Chelsea almost choked on her milk. Which story was true? Earlier she'd gotten the impression that Kesha's mom wasn't around much at all.

Mike pushed away from the table. "Excuse me. I'm gonna walk Gracie now." He turned to Kesha. "I'm taking care of a dog while her owner's away. For two weeks! I get to feed her and take her for walks and play with her."

"Want me to go with you?" Kesha asked excitedly.

Chelsea gasped. "You can't! I mean, we have plans, remember?"

Kesha grinned. "Sure . . . Okay . . . Maybe another day, Mike."

"Anytime." Mike flipped over and walked on his hands to the door. Grinning, he flipped back to his feet and walked out.

Kesha laughed. "I wish I could do that."

Chelsea jumped up. If she wasn't careful, Kesha would invite herself back until she learned to walk on her hands and got to walk Gracie . . . and maybe borrow everything in her closet! "Ready, Kesha?"

"Sure . . . I guess." Kesha followed Chelsea to the door but turned back with a smile. "It was nice meeting you, Mrs. McCrea. And you too, Rob."

"It was a delight to meet you, Kesha. Come whenever you can," Mom offered.

Chelsea's heart sank. Kesha would think that

gave her the right to move in! Chelsea hurried to the stairs and ran on up with Kesha slowly following. The smell of the brownies filled the hall.

In her room Chelsea flung her closet door open. She tapped her toe as she waited for Kesha. Where was she? Chelsea bit her lip and ran to the hall. Kesha was standing in the doorway of the master bedroom, looking in. The yearning on her face brought a lump to Chelsea's throat. Impatiently she forced back her pity. "Hurry, Kesha. You have a long way to walk home. Your family will be worried about you."

Kesha slowly turned. "They never care where I am. They don't know what I wear to school or what grades I get. They never sit at the table together and eat brownies and drink milk . . . or even have dinner together." Her voice broke. "I thought this kind of life was only make-believe—like on TV."

Chelsea's eyes pricked with tears for an instant, but then she remembered all Kesha had done today and she blinked the tears away. "Come look in my closet and see what you want to wear."

Kesha slowly walked toward Chelsea. "You mad at me?"

"No."

"Then what's wrong?"

"Well . . . it's just that . . . I've never done what we did today. It makes me feel guilty."

Kesha frowned. "Guilty? Why? That's really crazy, Chel Sea. I don't understand you at all!"

Chelsea didn't want to take the time to explain.

"I have dress pants that are a little long on me, but they should fit you just right."

"Great! What color?"

"Coral. And a coral top with white flowers."

"Show me." Kesha stood near the closet and looked eagerly inside.

Chelsea pulled out the pleated pants and the soft top. She hadn't even worn them yet. She held them close to her a minute but then handed them to Kesha.

"Oh, they're too beautiful, Chel Sea!" Kesha quickly pulled off her clothes and slipped on the slacks and top. They fit her perfectly. She gazed speechlessly in the mirror as she turned this way and that. She unhooked the lime-green clip and let her blonde curls fall to her shoulder and around her face.

Chelsea nodded. "The clothes look better on you than on me."

"I've never worn clothes like this before . . . ever!" Kesha gently touched the white flowers embroidered along the neckline of the top. "I never wore . . . new clothes." Her voice dropped to a whisper. "Not ever!"

Chelsea couldn't imagine that. She'd never worn anything but new clothes. Once in a while back in Oklahoma she'd shared clothes with Sidney, her very best friend, but they'd been clothes that only Sid had worn.

"I'll wear these clothes tomorrow." Kesha peered in the closet. "What about you, Chel?"

"I don't know. Probably jeans."

"Why wear jeans when you have dress pants that are so pretty?"

Chelsea pulled out a new pair of jeans and held them up.

Kesha's eyes widened. "Oh! You don't mean faded and ragged jeans!" Kesha touched the soft denim. "Maybe I should wear jeans . . ." She stepped in front of the mirror again and shook her head. "No, I'll wear this. But how can I carry them home?"

"In my book bag." Chelsea quickly emptied it and dropped it onto the bed.

Reluctantly Kesha took off the slacks and top and slipped on her clothes. She looked in the mirror. Slowly she lifted her curls and hooked the clip in place. "I wish I had clothes like you, Chel." With a laugh Kesha spun around to face Chelsea. "So who cares? I've got something pretty for tomorrow, right? That's more than I ever had before. I should be glad, right?"

Chelsea folded the slacks and top and carefully packed them in the bag. Would Kesha return them looking as nice? What if she ruined them? Chelsea's stomach tightened. It was too late to think of that now. She'd agreed to let Kesha borrow them. "I'll walk down the block with you."

"Great!" Kesha flipped her ponytail and tugged at her brightly colored top. "Let's go!"

Chelsea bit back a sigh of relief as she hurried down the stairs and out the front door with Kesha. Just as they started down the sidewalk the Best Friends ran up to them. Chelsea's skin burned as she tried to think of a way to make Kesha disappear. Reluctantly Chelsea introduced the girls to Kesha. The Best Friends told Kesha where they lived and asked her where she lived. As they talked, Chelsea moved restlessly from one foot to the other. A car drove past with music blaring out the open windows. Gracie barked in the backyard, and Mike laughed and called to her.

Rob ran out the door and called hello to the girls. He ran down the sidewalk toward the corner store where he sometimes worked stocking shelves or bagging groceries.

Chelsea looked longingly after Rob. Right now she'd rather be with him and away from Kesha and the Best Friends. What if Kesha told about their day? Chelsea shivered.

Hannah moved closer to Chelsea. "You're sure quiet, Chel."

She shrugged. "There's nothing to say."

"Are you all right?"

Chelsea suddenly wanted to tell Hannah *everything* about her miserable day, but she couldn't—not in front of Kesha.

Hannah leaned closer to Chelsea and whispered, "I'll talk to you later."

Chelsea nodded as she struggled against the hot tears burning the backs of her eyes.

Kesha turned to Hannah. "You should wear a beaded headband and a fringed leather jacket to show everybody you're proud to be Ottawa."

Hannah blinked in surprise. "I don't know . . . Everybody would stare at me."

"Of course! That's what you want, isn't it?" Kesha grinned. "Never look invisible! Right, Chel?"

Chelsea barely nodded.

Roxie giggled. "I like being invisible in social studies when I don't know the answer."

"Me too," Kathy said, laughing. "And science."

"I *love* science!" Kesha clasped the book bag to her chest. "I like knowing what makes everything work. Don't you ever wonder how the stars got in the sky?"

Kathy grinned. "I already know that. God created the earth, and He put the stars in the sky."

Kesha's eyes widened as she turned to Chelsea. "Is that true?"

Chelsea nodded.

"I never ever knew that! How'd He do it?"

"He spoke, and what He spoke happened," Hannah said.

"This is sooo incredible!"

Chelsea glanced at the Best Friends. They were looking at Kesha strangely. Chelsea nudged Kesha. "You said you have to get home."

"I know. But I don't want to leave yet."

Just then Mom walked out, her purse in her hand. "Chelsea, I have to run to the Post Office." Mom spotted Kesha. "I can give you a ride home, Kesha."

"That's great!"

Chelsea trembled. She couldn't leave Kesha alone with Mom! "I'll go too!" Chelsea turned to Hannah. "Will you watch Mike for me? Please!"

Hannah nodded. "I'll stay with Mike, Mrs. McCrea."

"That's nice of you. Thanks." Mom pulled her car keys out. "We won't be gone long."

Chelsea said a quick good-bye and ran to the car. She and Kesha climbed into the backseat.

"This is really great, Mrs. McCrea. I don't mind walking, of course, but riding is nice."

"Tell me exactly where you live." Mom backed out of the driveway and turned left according to Kesha's directions.

Chelsea locked her icy hands in her lap and looked straight ahead. She slowly relaxed as Kesha sat quietly.

Mom turned on Kesha's street and drove slowly down it.

Chelsea looked at the cluttered yards and the small, rundown houses.

"I live in the apartment building on the corner." Kesha leaned against the front seat. "We're still looking for a house. It's really terrible living in such a place when we're used to better."

Chelsea groaned at Kesha's lie.

"I'm sure you'll find something," Mom said, smiling.

Chelsea stared at the four-story apartment building. It was an ugly brown building with a paved parking area. Mom pulled into the parking area and let Kesha out.

"See you tomorrow, Chel." With the book bag in one hand, Kesha waved and ran to the side door.

Chelsea sank against the backseat and closed her eyes.

"She's a sweet girl," Mom said as she drove out of the parking area toward the Post Office. "I'm glad you're friends with her. She needs a friend."

Chelsea stiffened. "What do you mean?"

"She's very lonely. I could tell by the way she acted." Mom stopped outside the Post Office and glanced back at Chelsea. "Be on your guard with her, honey. She doesn't always tell the truth."

Chelsea leaned forward with a gasp. "How'd you know?"

"I just know." Mom smiled. "We'll pray for her. You be a good friend to her, Chelsea. Show her God's love."

Chelsea trembled. She hadn't even thought about doing that. She bit her lip. Could she show Kesha God's love? Did she even want to?

7

Chel Sea and Kesha

Her heart racing, Chelsea walked slowly up to the Best Friends who sat on the front steps as Mom hurried into the house. Chelsea had thought only Hannah would be there, but Kathy and Roxie had stayed too. Taking a deep breath, Chelsea said, "Hi."

"We've been talking about you." Roxie patted a spot beside her. "Sit down."

Chelsea sank to the step. She wanted to run to her room, but she knew the girls would follow her to find out what was wrong.

Kathy twirled a flower in her hand. "We've been wondering about Kesha."

She knew they would be, but she still stiffened. "What about her?"

"She seems . . . different. Not a girl you'd choose for a friend, Chelsea." Hannah twisted her long dark hair around and around her long dark finger.

Roxie stamped her foot. "Chel, we want to know about you and Kesha."

72

Frantically Chelsea searched for the words to say. "Well, I don't know . . . What about us?"

The Best Friends exchanged wondering looks.

"Whatever it is, we want to help." Hannah looked ready to cry.

"We're friends, Chel." Kathy wrapped her hands around her knees. "We'll do anything for you!"

Chelsea's eyes flashed. "Like let me go back to my own school in Oklahoma?"

Kathy flushed. "We can't do that."

"We don't want you to go back!" Hannah cried. "You're my first friend ever! I couldn't go back to having no friends!" She flushed and looked sheepishly at Kathy and Roxie. "You're my friends too, and I think you're both really great, but Chelsea was my first friend. You understand, don't you?"

"Sure," Kathy and Roxie said together.

"You were dressed so . . . strange today." Hannah touched Chelsea's arm. "You looked great, but it just wasn't you."

"How did you have the nerve to do it?" Kathy asked.

Chelsea shrugged. She wanted to tell them just how hard it had been, but she couldn't.

"And we heard some really strange stories about you, Chel. Like . . . well, like you had some kind of problem and had to have help in the restroom." Roxie looked down at the grass, then over at Chelsea.

Her head spun, and she couldn't answer.

Hannah took a deep breath. "Susan Kemp's sister from church said you were in the eighth grade photography class with Kesha. She said you made Mr. Scott think you were eighth graders."

Chelsea's heart felt like a giant chunk of ice. "You know how stories spread even when they aren't true." Her voice was weak and shaky.

"I know." Roxie nodded. "My sister Lacy said when she was a freshman someone spread a story that she was kissing a boy in the hall. She wasn't, but lots of kids believed the story. I told her I would've believed her just because I know her."

Chelsea burned with shame. Her friends didn't want to believe anything bad about her. *She* didn't want to believe anything bad about herself, but she knew the truth.

Just then the door opened, and Chelsea's mom called her to come in to help with dinner. In relief Chelsea jumped up, said a quick good-bye, and ran inside. She couldn't face the Best Friends a minute longer or she'd break down and tell them all the terrible things she'd done with Kesha today.

At dinner Chelsea ate slowly as she listened to Dad tell about his day at work. She didn't want him to ask her about hers like he usually did. The phone rang at the end of the meal, and Dad answered. It was Grandpa McCrea. Chelsea breathed a sigh of relief. Grandpa didn't call very often, but when he did he stayed on a long time. She helped clean the kitchen and then hurried to her room. Tonight she wouldn't watch TV or play games with the family but would just read in her room.

Two days ago she'd started the new *Sadie Rose* book. She picked it up and curled up on her bed. She opened it and started to read, but the words were only words instead of an exciting story. The incidents of the day whirled around and around her brain until she thought her head would spin right off her shoulders.

Finally she took a shower and dressed in her Oklahoma T-shirt that reached to her knees. Listlessly she dried her hair. The fine strands of red hair danced in the hot air.

Later she read her Bible but didn't even know what she read. She prayed, but it was all just words. With a whimper she crawled between the sheets and closed her eyes.

Just then her door opened. She blinked against the hall light. She smelled Dad's aftershave.

"We came to say good night." Dad bent down and kissed her cheek. "Grandpa said to say hi. Grandma too. They miss you a lot and wish they could see you."

Chelsea smiled. She loved Grandpa and Grandma McCrea.

Mom kissed Chelsea. "You're a blessed girl. God is always with you."

Tears stung Chelsea's eyes. "Good night," she whispered hoarsely. She watched Mom and Dad walk out and close the door quietly behind them. Sighing in relief, she sank into her pillow and closed her eyes. Maybe she'd fall asleep, and the long, horrible day would stop repeating itself.

The next morning she slowly crawled out of bed, yawning and blurry-eyed. She'd dreamed the teachers had sent her and Kesha to the principal's office, where they'd been paddled and scolded. She rubbed her eyes and yawned again. She'd never been sent to the office, nor had she ever been spanked by a teacher or a principal, but Grandpa had told her about being paddled many times in school when he was a boy. He'd said the paddle was a board full of holes with a handle. The holes made the spanking hurt more. She shivered. She could still feel the paddling from her dream.

Slowly she dressed in her good jeans, a blue-and-cream top, and sneakers. She combed her long hair and then held it back on each side with two wide barrettes. She stood in front of the mirror and studied herself. She looked very different than she had yesterday. "I wish yesterday had never happened," she muttered as she turned away from the full-length mirror.

The phone rang, and she jumped. She answered it even though she was sure it was for Mom. It was Kesha! Chelsea gripped the phone and sank to her chair.

"Did I wake you up, Chel Sea?"

"No. I'm going to breakfast now."

"Breakfast? I never eat breakfast."

"Why are you calling?"

Kesha was quiet a long time.

Chelsea frowned. "Kesha?"

"I'm afraid I'll look dumb in your clothes."

"What? You looked gorgeous in them! What do you mean, 'dumb'?"

Kesha giggled. "I never wore ordinary pants and top before. I always dress . . . you know . . . like I did yesterday."

Chelsea shook her head. "Kesha, dress the way you want. I'm wearing jeans and a blue-and-cream top."

"You're right. Why should I be scared? I'll wear your stuff. If anybody makes fun of me, they'll be sooo sorry!"

"Nobody will make fun of you." Chelsea rolled her eyes. "Don't be so nervous."

"You're right! See you later!"

"See ya." Chelsea hung up and ran downstairs to the kitchen. It seemed strange to think Kesha was afraid to dress in ordinary clothes.

"Morning, Chelsea. You look beautiful again today."

She didn't feel beautiful. "Thanks."

Mom sat alone at the table with a cup of tea and toast. "The boys are already gone. They had friends to meet."

Chelsea glanced at her watch. "I'd better hurry." She fixed a bowl of cornflakes and sat at the table.

"Who was on the phone?"

"Kesha. She was worried about what to wear today."

"Invite her to dinner sometime, Chel."

Chelsea filled her mouth with cornflakes so she wouldn't have to answer.

Mom stuck her cup and saucer in the dishwasher and picked up her purse. "I have to go now, Chel. See you after school. Be sure the house is locked when you leave."

Chelsea nodded as she chewed. She heard the door close after Mom. Chelsea dropped her spoon in her empty bowl. Excitement rushed through her. Why, she wouldn't even have to go to school! She could stay home all alone. Nobody would know.

She frowned. Who was she kidding? The teachers would let Mom and Dad know, and they'd punish her.

Chelsea loaded her bowl and spoon in the dishwasher and hurried out the door, checking to see that it was locked behind her. She ran down the sidewalk toward the street outside The Ravines. The sidewalks were empty. Had she already missed the bus? In the distance she heard the bus coming. She raced up to the other kids and reached them just as the bus stopped with a hiss of brakes.

As she glanced around for Hannah or Roxie, someone caught her arm. She turned to find Kesha there.

"How do I look?" Kesha whispered.

Over the noise of the boys and girls Chelsea looked Kesha up and down. The slacks and top looked like they'd been made just for her. "Like I told you yesterday . . . you look great."

"Well, I wasn't sure." Kesha giggled. "I had to hear you say it again."

"I see you didn't dye your hair red."

"I decided not to yet. Maybe tonight."

Chelsea stepped up into the bus with Kesha close behind.

Roxie waved from near the back and called, "Chel, right here!"

"She's sitting with me," Kesha called back to Roxie.

Chelsea pressed her lips tightly together. Did Kesha think she was going to make her do everything her way again?

Kesha pushed Chelsea into an empty seat and dropped down beside her. "I wish I lived in The Ravines. I had to get up really early to get here in time for the bus."

"But you called me just a while ago."

"I know. From the corner store where your brother works. I told the woman there I was your friend, and she let me use her phone instead of the pay phone. Wasn't that nice of her?"

"Real nice." Chelsea locked her hands in her lap and tried to block out Kesha's chatter.

Later in their homeroom Chelsea opened her reading book.

"Do you like to read out loud?" Kesha whispered.

Chelsea shrugged. "I don't feel like it today."

Kesha raised her hand high and waved it.

"Yes, Kesha," Mr. Borgman said in his gravelly voice.

"Chel Sea's having trouble with her eyes. She was too embarrassed to say so. So I'll read in her place when it's her turn to read."

Her face burning, Chelsea wanted to vanish into thin air.

Mr. Borgman shrugged. "Do you need to see the school nurse, Chelsea?"

She shook her head.

"Then let's start reading. Kesha, suppose you read the first two pages since you so willingly volunteered."

In a ringing voice Kesha read the two pages. When she finished she looked smug.

After class, out in the crowded hall, Chelsea turned to Kesha. "Why'd you say I had eye problems?"

Kesha shrugged and smiled brightly. "You said you didn't want to read. I was only helping you out."

"Well, don't help me again!"

Kesha's face fell. "Why not? We're friends. I was gonna get us out of math class again too."

"No! I mean it, Kesha."

"Oh, all right, but I don't understand you at all."

Chelsea hurried to math class with Kesha staying close at her side. Just as they sat down, a voice over the intercom said, "Chelsea McCrea and Kesha Bronski, report to the principal's office immediately."

Chelsea's heart zoomed to her feet. The office!

She'd never ever been called out of class to go to the office. She scowled at Kesha.

"At least it'll get us out of math," Kesha whispered with a grin.

Chelsea ducked her head and walked into the hall. She knew the Best Friends were wondering what was happening. By the end of the day everyone in the entire school would know she'd been called to the office and why. She trembled.

"Don't be worried, Chel Sea. It's no big deal."

"It is to me," Chelsea snapped.

Kesha's lower lip quivered. "Are you mad at me?"

Without answering Chelsea hurried to the office. At the door, shivers ran over her. Her legs felt too weak to hold her.

"Let me handle it." Kesha opened the door and boldly stepped inside. She marched right to the desk and said, "I'm Kesha Bronski, and this is Chel Sea McCrea. We were in Mrs. Williams's math class, and someone called us out—we don't know why."

Chelsea bit her lip and tried not to look as frightened as she felt. If this were Grandpa's day, she'd be paddled. What punishment did they give students now?

"Mrs. Evans is expecting you." The woman motioned to a closed door to her left. "Go right on in."

Kesha walked straight to the door and opened it. She lifted her chin and walked in.

Chelsea hesitated and then followed her.

"Kesha and Chel Sea to see you, Mrs. Evans." Kesha smiled a wide smile that showed off her white teeth.

Mrs. Evans motioned for them to sit down in the gold plastic chairs across from her. She was in her thirties and wore a gray suit and peach-colored blouse. She wasn't smiling. "I've been hearing stories about the two of you."

"Excellent ones, we hope." Smiling, Kesha crossed her legs and stroked the soft fabric of her borrowed pants.

Chelsea gripped the arms of the chair and kept her feet firmly on the floor.

Mrs. Evans slowly walked around her desk. She looked down at Kesha and Chelsea. "I've called both your parents."

Chelsea bit back a groan.

Kesha's smile faded. "Did you get them?"

Mrs. Evans leaned back against her desk and crossed her arms. "Chelsea, I reached your mom at work. I explained why you'd been called to the office. Kesha, I couldn't reach your parents—neither of them."

"I could take a note home to them." Kesha fingered the barrette that held back her blonde curls. "If you want, that is."

"I'll continue to try to reach them, but if I don't by the end of the school day, I will indeed send a note home with you." Mrs. Evans sighed heavily and walked back to her chair. "I can't believe you two girls could take such liberties as you did yesterday. Chelsea, we know you aren't suffering with any kind of disorder. You're in good health, according to your records and according to your mother. What do you have to say for yourself, young lady?"

Chelsea shrugged. Every word she'd ever learned was suddenly locked tightly inside her frozen brain.

"She's really sorry," Kesha said. "You really shouldn't blame her at all. You see, she was nervous about a new school. Me? I'm used to 'em, so I helped her have a good day."

"I see." Mrs. Evans picked up a yellow pencil and tapped it against her open notebook. "You girls realize you'll have detention, don't you?"

Kesha shrugged.

Chelsea blinked back tears. Detention! That was only for kids who were really bad. Now everyone would think she was one of the bad students. This was too terrible for words.

"You'll eat your lunch quickly, then return to your homeroom for the remainder of the lunch period. You may not speak to each other or write notes back and forth. Mr. Murphy will assign you extra work, and you'll do it. If you don't finish your work, days will be added to your detention. Have I made myself clear?"

"Yes, ma'am, you certainly have. Me and Chel Sea will do just what you said. Won't we?"

Chelsea nodded.

"You girls return to your math class. Here's a

pass." Mrs. Evans scribbled on a pad, tore off the top sheet, and handed it to Kesha. "If you break any more rules, you'll be suspended. Don't let that happen."

Chelsea hung her head as she followed Kesha from the room.

In the hall Kesha giggled as she waved the pass. "That wasn't so bad, was it?"

"Bad? It was terrible!"

Kesha looked closely at Chelsea. "Are you upset?"

"Yes!"

"I'm sure sorry. It's really no big deal."

"Maybe not to you, but it is to me!"

Kesha frowned slightly. "I don't understand you, Chel. We had a great time yesterday. You got a lot of attention, and you didn't have to stay in the classes you didn't like."

"Now we're paying for it!"

"Only with detention. It's not like they're going to cut off our fingers or burn a brand on our cheeks like we read about one time in history."

Chelsea studied Kesha and finally nodded. Kesha was right. Things really weren't as bad as she'd thought. So what if she had detention? It really wasn't a big deal. She laughed a shaky little laugh.

"I think I will dye my hair red." Kesha slipped her hand through Chelsea's arm as they walked toward math class. "Want to help me?"

"Sure . . . I guess so."

"I'll come to your house after I get the dye, and we'll do it there."

Chelsea giggled. It might be fun to dye Kesha's hair. "You know, I might even dye mine . . . Maybe black. Wouldn't that look great?"

"If it makes you happy, Chel."

"It just might!" Chelsea grinned, then opened the door to the math room and walked on in.

8

Detention

Chelsea sat in math class with her head high. The room was so hot that her jeans clung to her legs. The mixed smells of perfume and sweat turned her stomach. She forced a smile. She was not going to let anyone think she was a terrible person just because she'd been called out of class. No one knew she had to be in detention. Not yet anyway. Even if they did, they wouldn't know why she was there. No one would ever think she'd do anything bad. Would they?

A yellow pencil in her hand, Kesha sat quietly beside her.

"Kesha, come up and work this problem on the board." Mrs. Williams pointed with a piece of chalk.

"Be glad to!" Kesha walked with her shoulders square and her chin high. She smiled at Mrs. Williams, then started to work the problem.

"I almost didn't recognize you, Kesha," Mrs. Williams said. "You look very nice."

A boy whistled a wolf whistle. Chelsea knotted her fists, but Kesha acted as if she didn't hear it.

Smiling, Kesha turned to face Mrs. Williams. "Thank you. Chel Sea and I decided to dress in regular clothes instead of wild ones."

Chelsea groaned. Why couldn't Kesha keep quiet?

"That's fine." Mrs. Williams motioned to the blackboard. "Finish the problem."

Kesha smiled. "We thought you and the other teachers would like us better."

"It's not a matter of like or dislike." Mrs. Williams cleared her throat. "Some clothes shout rebellion, and others don't. Yours seemed to be designed for attention and daring."

Kesha looked at Mrs. Williams thoughtfully. "I never looked at it that way. I just knew I had fun wearing clothes that made me different from others. But I like dressing this way even better. I feel . . . grand!"

Chelsea sank low in her seat, while the students roared with laughter. Kesha talked way too much!

Kesha frowned. "What did I say? I feel very dressed up. There's nothing wrong with that."

"Nothing indeed." Mrs. Williams patted Kesha's shoulder. "Work the problem, and take your seat."

Chelsea wanted to glance around to see how the Best Friends were looking at Kesha, but she couldn't find the strength even to turn her head. Couldn't Kesha ever keep her mouth shut?

During science Chelsea read the pages assigned and took a short quiz. She didn't do very well, but Kesha got 100 percent.

After science Chelsea hesitantly followed Kesha to the cafeteria. Smells of spaghetti and meatballs overpowered all the other smells in the hall.

Hannah caught Chelsea's arm and hurried along with her. "Why were you called to the office? Is something wrong?"

Embarrassed, Chelsea couldn't look at Hannah. "Mrs. Evans scolded me for being out of class and some other things."

"And?"

Her whole insides knotted tightly, Chelsea forced a smile. "And I have to go to detention for the rest of the week."

"Oh, Chelsea!" Hannah's eyes filled with tears. "I'm really really sorry."

Chelsea's face hardened. "About what?"

Hannah's eyes widened. "The call to the office!"

"It wasn't anything at all."

"Oh, Chel, it must have been terrible for you."

"I said it wasn't anything!" Anger rose in Chelsea. "Just leave me alone." She pulled away from Hannah and ran after Kesha, who was already in line.

"What kept you, Chel?"

"Nothing." Chelsea glanced back to find Hannah, but couldn't see her among the crowd of noisy students. Why had she hurt Hannah like that? Hannah was always kind and thoughtful, even when she was feeling bad at being treated unkindly because she was Ottawa. Chelsea wanted to slam her tray to the floor and cry out at the top of her lungs. Everything was going wrong! And it was all because she'd been forced to attend this new school!

"Kesha! Chel! Sit with us!" Three girls at a table waved to Kesha and Chelsea.

Kesha headed right for them, but Chelsea hung back. The girls looked like they belonged to a gang or something. All three had short brown hair and dirty fingernails. Chelsea started for a different table, but Kesha turned around and called to her. Reluctantly she joined Kesha and the girls.

"So, do you have detention?" asked one girl who wore an old leather jacket.

"Sure do." Kesha took a big bite of spaghetti.

Chelsea sipped her juice to relieve the dryness in her mouth.

"We got it too." The girl laughed. "We got caught smoking in the restroom. I'm Tilly, and that's Gina and Lucile," she told Chelsea.

Lucile wrinkled her nose. "Smoking! What's wrong with that? Nothing worth gettin' detention for."

"You girls been smoking too?" Gina asked.

"No!" Chelsea cried, shaking her head hard.

Kesha grinned. "We skipped class."

Chelsea almost choked on her bite of food. Oh, how she wished she could totally wipe out yesterday! But she couldn't; what was done was done.

"We skipped class too, but nobody caught us," Tilly said with a chuckle.

Chelsea suddenly lost the tiny bit of appetite she'd had. She barely managed to finish her juice.

A few minutes later she slowly walked behind Kesha and the three girls to detention. Chelsea hesitated outside the room. Chelsea McCrea in detention? Unthinkable!

Chelsea glanced around the room, which was empty except for two boys sitting near the window. They looked up, then back out the window. Gina ran to the boys and talked to them excitedly. They laughed and joked with her. Chelsea shuddered at the bad words they kept using.

Kesha jabbed Chelsea in the arm and whispered, "Don't act like such a snob or the others will be mean to you."

Chelsea sank to a seat and groaned. She wasn't a snob! She just wasn't used to being around kids like the others in the room. How could she act like she was happy to be with them?

A man in his late twenties walked in and sat at the desk without looking around. "I'm Mr. Murphy. I'll be in here with you. I don't want trouble from any of you." He looked up and blinked in surprise at seeing Chelsea and Kesha. "This is detention. Are you girls supposed to be in here?"

Chelsea wanted to shout, "No!" But she knew she had to stay there.

"I'm Kesha Bronski, and this is Chel Sea McCrea."

Mr. Murphy looked at his paper and nodded.

"I'm surprised to see you two in here." He looked at the others. "Come get your work sheets. No cheating. No talking. Hand the work in when the bell rings."

Chelsea read over the work sheets and groaned. It was a little of everything. The last assignment was to write a paragraph on why she wouldn't be in detention again. She shuddered as she realized someone would be reading her paragraph. She glanced at Kesha. She was acting as if she were in an ordinary class. How could she do that?

Her hands clammy and her heart racing, Chelsea answered most of the questions, skipped the few she didn't know, and finally started the final paragraph. She wrote:

> I will never be in detention again because I won't break the rules. I didn't think about breaking rules or being put in detention. This is a new school for me, and I couldn't get used to being here. Kesha is new too. She said she'd help me. She wants to be my friend. But does a friend get you in trouble? I don't think so. But Kesha doesn't feel that way. She thinks she's doing me a big favor by making me act like she does. She doesn't even know it's wrong to skip class or tell lies. I guess it was nice of her to try to help me. After this I will think and act for myself. I won't let anyone talk me into doing something wrong, no matter how scared or lonely I am. If I never

break rules, I won't be sent to detention. And I don't plan to be in detention ever again as long as I live.

The bell rang, and Chelsea jumped up. She couldn't wait to get out of there! She handed in her paper and rushed out of the room and away from the three girls who were clustered around Kesha.

Just outside the room Kathy stopped Chelsea. Kathy looked worried. "Are you all right, Chel?"

Her body pricking with embarrassment, she nodded.

"I heard you had detention." Kathy bit her lip and looked sad. "Did you?"

Chelsea barely nodded.

"Oh, Chel, I'm sorry . . . What can I do to help you?"

"I don't know," Chelsea whispered hoarsely. She wanted to run away from Kathy. "I have to get to English class."

"I'll walk with you."

Hot tears stung Chelsea's eyes as she walked with Kathy into English class.

"You're special to God," Kathy whispered.

Chelsea sank to her desk. She wasn't special at all! She was a total failure!

Kesha dropped to her seat and leaned toward Chelsea. "We'll have to be careful of those three girls—Tilly, Lucile, and Gina. They're out to make trouble in detention tomorrow."

Chelsea shivered. "How?"

"I don't know yet."

"Let's tell Mr. Murphy."

"You kidding? We can't do that!" Kesha frowned. "Promise you won't do that, Chel."

She barely nodded. What did it matter anyway? It wouldn't affect her one way or the other.

"What are you wearing to school tomorrow?"

Chelsea shrugged. That was way at the bottom of her list of things to think about.

"I guess I have to give your clothes back to you." Kesha sounded like she didn't want to.

Chelsea nodded. Mom would be very upset if Kesha kept the clothes. They'd cost a lot of money.

Just then the boy in front of Chelsea turned around and said, "I hear you got detention for doing drugs."

Chelsea gasped and shook her head.

"We skipped class," Kesha snapped. "We don't do drugs."

The boy grinned and turned around.

Chelsea's ears burned. Did others think she did drugs?

After class two girls stopped Chelsea and Kesha. "Why'd you get detention?" the tallest girl asked.

The other girl said, "I heard you got caught with a knife in your locker."

A boy listening to them said, "I heard Chelsea stole money from the office."

In agony Chelsea stared down at the floor. How

could the students believe such terrible things about her?

Kesha knotted her fists and narrowed her eyes. "We skipped class—that's all. So don't go making up something worse!"

Just then Chelsea looked up. She saw Roxie standing nearby. She'd heard everything! But what would she believe? What would she tell Kathy and Hannah?

Chelsea slowly turned and walked away. A dark cloud settled over her and seemed to squeeze the life right out of her body.

9

A Talk with Mom and Dad

Chelsea stood in her yard and looked at her house. Mom was waiting inside, and she knew *everything*!

His face red and his auburn hair tangled, Rob ran to Chelsea. "I can't believe you got sent to detention for having a knife in your locker! Where'd you ever get a knife?"

Chelsea fell back a step. "Rob, I never had a knife!"

"Pete Bromberg said you did."

Chelsea stumbled to the steps and sat down. "I can't believe you thought it was true," she whispered as tears slowly filled her eyes. Never in her wildest imaginings would she think Rob would believe anything bad of her!

Rob flushed as he sat beside her. "I thought maybe someone gave you a knife for some strange reason and you stuck it in your locker."

She shook her head.

"Then why were you in . . . detention?"

She told him. "It was really really awful, Rob."

"I can't believe you'd even let Kesha do that to you."

"I know. It just . . . happened."

Rob shook his head. "Chel, things don't just happen. You let Kesha take over your life."

Chelsea jumped up and doubled her fists. "What do you know, Robert McCrea? It wasn't my fault we moved here! It wasn't my fault we had to go to a new school! Everyone there treated me like I was invisible! I hated that! Kesha said she'd help me. She was new too, so I believed her. It wasn't my fault at all!" Chelsea ran into the house and started up the stairs.

"Chelsea!"

She froze at the sound of Mom's stern voice. Slowly she turned. The strength left her body, and she gripped the banister so she could stay on her feet.

Mom slowly walked toward Chelsea. "I'm very sorry for what happened to you today. It'll be hard for me, but I'll wait until your father gets home before we talk about it. I called him at work, and he knows what happened. You change your clothes and get your chores done. After dinner we'll talk."

Chelsea nodded.

"I love you, Chelsea. I'm sorry for what you did. It was wrong. But *I love you*."

Tears blurred Chelsea's eyes. "Oh, Mom, it was so awful!"

Mom pulled Chelsea into her arms and held her. She clung to Mom and sobbed against her shoulder.

Her eyes wet with tears, Mom held Chelsea away from her and looked into her face. "This hurts me as much as it does you, but we'll get through it with strength from God."

"I wish we'd stayed in Oklahoma."

Mom's chin quivered. "But we didn't. We're here, and we can be happy. We can be a blessing to people around us."

Chelsea bit her lip. She knew Mom hadn't wanted to move any more than she had. But Mom had adjusted. She'd found a job she liked, and Kathy Aber's mom was her best friend.

Mom gently rubbed a strand of hair off Chelsea's cheek. "How do Kesha's parents feel about what happened?"

"Mrs. Evans couldn't get them on the phone, so she sent a note home with Kesha."

Mom shook her head. "She probably won't give it to them."

"Mom! How can you say that?"

"I wasn't born yesterday."

Chelsea frowned. Mom always said that when she meant she knew a lot more than others thought. "What'll she do then?"

"Probably write a note to the school and sign her mom's name. Does her mom even live with her? I think we should find out more about little Kesha Bronski."

"Oh, Mom, don't do that! Please. She'd be really upset."

"I don't think she would, Chelsea. I think Kesha is crying out for help."

Chelsea shook her head. "She's not, Mom."

"Run upstairs and change." Mom kissed Chelsea's cheek and then swatted her bottom. "Run along."

Chelsea slowly walked upstairs, her hand on the smooth banister. Mom was totally wrong about Kesha. She didn't want to be any different than she already was.

After dinner Chelsea slowly walked to the study. Rob and Mike had gone to the park. Chelsea shivered. Dad had kissed her when he got home, had made jokes at dinner, had listened to the boys, but hadn't said a word about detention. He was saving it all for the big after-dinner meeting.

Chelsea heard Mom and Dad talking inside the study. The door was almost closed. Maybe they weren't ready for her.

"I hate for her to be in detention," Chelsea heard her mom say.

"So do I. I wish I could spare her that."

Chelsea's eyes widened. They didn't want her to have to be in detention! Maybe they'd get her out. Maybe she should let them make plans by themselves. She started to turn away, then stopped. She couldn't walk away. They'd find her and talk to her. This wasn't something they'd shrug off like they did if she spilled her milk or accidentally dropped a plate and broke it.

Sighing, Chelsea walked in. Mom and Dad were standing in the middle of the room with their arms around each other. They smiled at Chelsea and kissed each other. Then Mom walked to the sofa, and Dad waited for Chelsea. He rubbed a finger over his mustache and narrowed his blue eyes.

"I understand you had a bad couple of days," Dad said as he hugged Chelsea. "Sit by your mom, and we'll talk about it."

Chelsea smelled his aftershave and a hint of onion on his breath. She wanted to stay in the warmth of his arms, but she slowly walked to the sofa and sat in the corner, her arm flung over the armrest, her ankles crossed.

Dad leaned back on the desk with his hands on either side. His blue plaid shirt was tucked neatly into his pleated jeans. "I'm sorry about what's been happening to you. If I'd seen how upset you were about going to a new school, I would have tried harder to help you adjust."

"Me too." Mom reached over and patted Chelsea's leg.

"But we can't take all the blame." Dad shook his head. "You let Kesha lead you astray. Chelsea, you become just like whoever you hang out with."

She bit her lip. She'd heard this many times already, but this was the first time she'd ever hung out with someone who'd brought her this kind of trouble.

Dad walked to a chair and sat on the edge of it with his hands locked lightly between his knees. "You need to be strong enough to say no to something that's wrong. Skipping class was wrong. Letting lies pass as the truth was wrong. But you know that already, don't you?"

Her heart heavy, Chelsea barely nodded.

"But you can't abandon Kesha either. What you can do is to be strong enough to influence her for good. Don't let her drag you down; instead, pull her up."

"Maybe she wants to stay where she is." Chelsea's voice shook, and she cleared her throat. "She seems really happy."

"She's not," Mom said softly. "I saw sadness in her eyes . . . and a great loneliness."

Chelsea looked from Mom to Dad. "But how can I help her?"

"By being a true friend." Dad sat back in the chair. "And by helping her find Jesus as her Savior."

Chelsea barely nodded.

Mom ran her finger over Chelsea's hand. "If Kesha wants to skip class, talk her out of it. If she starts to tell a lie, stop her and tell the truth."

"I don't know if I can do that."

"Sure, you can . . . with God's help," Dad said gently.

"It would be a lot easier if I didn't have to go to detention." Chelsea waited, eager for them to jump in and say they'd handle that.

Dad nodded. "Yes, it would be easier."

"But you *are* in detention," Mom said, brushing a tear off her cheek.

Chelsea took a deep, unsteady breath. "Maybe you could talk to Mrs. Evans and get her to let me off. It really wasn't my fault."

Frowning, Dad leaned forward. "Whose fault was it?"

Chelsea laced her fingers together. "Maybe yours a little, for making us move."

"And?"

"And Kesha's for forcing me to do what she said."

"Anyone else?"

Chelsea nodded. "Everyone at the school! They acted like I wasn't even there!"

"I see." Dad glanced at Mom, then back at Chelsea. "And where do you fit in? Was any of it *your* fault?"

Chelsea heard the stern sound in Dad's voice. What did he expect of her?

A muscle jumped in Mom's cheek. "Was it, Chelsea?"

"Well, I suppose, but . . ."

Dad stabbed his fingers through his hair and then smoothed it down again. "Chelsea, you have to take responsibility for your own actions. Going to a new school is very traumatic, I admit, but that doesn't give you a good reason to sin."

Mom swallowed hard. "Lying is a sin. Breaking rules is wrong."

"But I only did them because of Kesha!"

Dad shook his head. "No, Chelsea, you did them because you chose to. You could've said no to Kesha. Jesus was right there to help you, but you didn't ask for His help. You used your own strength—which wasn't enough. Always remember that Jesus is your Friend and Savior. God is your Heavenly Father. The Holy Spirit is your helper and comforter. You are never alone!"

Chelsea knew that what Dad said was the truth. She had been wrong. She had gone her own way without God's help. But no more! The hard band around her heart finally snapped. Tears filled her eyes. "I was wrong," she whispered. "I'm sooo sorry!"

Dad pulled her to her feet and put an arm around her and another around Mom. The three of them stood in the middle of the study in a tight, warm hug. Dad prayed, then Mom did, and finally Chelsea.

After a long time Chelsea wiped the tears from her eyes and smiled. Once again she was the real Chelsea McCrea—the Chelsea McCrea made in the image of God—the new creature in Christ. And now that's what she wanted for Kesha.

Chelsea smiled. "I'll help Kesha . . . starting tomorrow."

Mom shook her head. "Starting right now . . . by praying for her."

Chelsea nodded. Once again she bowed her head with Mom and Dad, and they all three prayed for Kesha.

10

Help from the Best Friends

Chelsea sat cross-legged on her bed with the Best Friends around her. She had told them everything, even what Mom and Dad had said. She had apologized to Hannah and Kathy for being mean to them. They had agreed to help with Kesha. Now Chelsea was waiting to hear the plan they'd all follow. A pleasant breeze blew in the window, bringing in the smell of fresh air. The only sounds were the curtains fluttering and Roxie chewing her gum.

"It's too late to visit Kesha tonight." Kathy tapped her bottom lip with her finger. "So we can't talk to her."

Roxie leaned forward eagerly. "Unless you have her phone number."

"I don't. But I know where she lives . . . In an apartment building on Spruce Street." Chelsea told

103

them about her mom taking Kesha home. "It's a poor part of town."

"Remember Mary Harland?" Roxie pushed her gum into her cheek with her tongue. "She lives in a poor part of town too. It made me sad to see their tiny house and all the rundown houses around."

Kathy looked thoughtful. "I wonder if our houses look rundown to Betina Quinn? Her house is such a mansion! I'd like to live in a mansion if I didn't have to clean it. That would be too much work."

"Do you know that some kids never have to help around the house?" Hannah shook her head. "I heard a girl complain because she had to unload the dishwasher once a day. Unload the dishwasher! All of us have to do a lot more than that."

"And we all have to baby-sit." Kathy wrinkled her nose. "I wonder if Kesha ever has to baby-sit."

"She has two younger brothers." Chelsea couldn't imagine having two brothers like Mike.

"Maybe Kesha will come here in the morning again." Hannah's dark eyes sparkled. "We could all talk to her then."

"Good idea," Roxie and Kathy said at the same time.

Chelsea looked toward her closet. "Kesha does have to bring back my clothes. So I do think she'll come in the morning." Suddenly Chelsea laughed. "I have an absolutely brilliant idea!"

"What?" the others asked all at once.

"Kesha doesn't have many clothes. Why don't we

each give her one outfit? We're all about the same size. We could ask our moms and see if that's okay."

Kathy nodded. "We did agree to do good deeds. I say let's do it!"

"I like it." Roxie grinned. She hadn't been so willing to do good deeds at first, but she'd been trying harder to act like Jesus wanted her to, and it was working.

"I say yes." Hannah giggled. "I could give her what she said I should wear—a beaded headband and a fringed leather jacket. And we could call her Ottawa."

Chelsea giggled along with the others. "I'll give her the outfit I wore to school Tuesday—the one she put together for me." The smiled faded. "But I don't think she wants to dress that way anymore. I think she'd rather look like us. Do you know she's never had new clothes to wear?"

"I've worn some of Lacy's old clothes, but I have my own things too." Roxie rubbed a hand down her jeans. "I wonder how it would feel never to have new things."

"With my closet so full I forget there are girls who don't have anything but rags to wear." Chelsea pulled her knees up to her chin. "I wish we could make sure everyone has things to wear."

"And to eat," Kathy said. "There are kids who don't have enough to eat. Even kids who starve to death!"

Hannah shivered. "My great-grandma tells stories about Ottawas starving to death. I'm glad my dad has a good job. I wouldn't want to ever be hungry and not have anything to eat."

"Maybe Kesha doesn't have enough to eat." Chelsea told them how hungry Kesha was at lunchtimes. "She said she never eats breakfast. She always seems to have money for a simple lunch, but maybe she doesn't have enough food at home."

"That's really really sad." Roxie looked ready to cry. "I sometimes wonder if my friend Mary Harland and her family have enough to eat. I see Mary's brother Dan sometimes when he takes Lacy out, and I wonder. It would be sooo sad to know someone who's going hungry."

"Especially when we throw away so much food," Hannah said. "My little sisters don't always feel like eating. But if they didn't have anything to eat they'd eat vegetables without complaining, I bet."

"I'm getting hungry." Kathy looked around. "You got anything to eat, Chel?"

Laughing, Chelsea shook her head. "We could go to the kitchen for cookies or apples. But first let's decide what to do for Kesha."

"We'll talk to her and tell her we'll be friends with her," Roxie suggested.

Kathy added, "We can tell her Jesus loves her."

"We'll tell her it's wrong to skip class and lie," Hannah added.

Chelsea listened to them while she thought about

Kesha. "I don't know if she'll listen to us. She likes to do things her way."

"She'll be glad to know Jesus loves her," Hannah said softly.

Chelsea agreed.

Roxie slid off the bed and stood beside it. "Did Kesha really have drugs in her locker?"

Chelsea frowned. "No!"

"That's what I heard. I'm glad it wasn't true." Roxie moved restlessly. "How do you know it's not true, Chel?"

Chelsea thought about that a while. "I don't know—I just know! She would've said something—wouldn't she?"

Roxie shrugged.

"You really don't know her." Hannah slipped off the bed. "Three days isn't much time to get to know someone."

Chelsea didn't want to believe Kesha would have drugs, but she knew Hannah was right—three days wasn't long enough to really get to know someone. "I won't believe about the drugs unless I see for myself."

"I say the same," Kathy said as she straightened the bedspread and put the pillows back in place. "Different stories have spread all over the school. We shouldn't believe any of them."

Roxie agreed. "But we can't just say Kesha is perfect either. We have to be careful so she doesn't fool us—especially you, Chelsea."

"She won't fool me." Chelsea shivered. But what if she did? "Come on, let's go downstairs."

Chelsea led the way to the kitchen. It smelled like lemons. She opened the cookie jar and pointed to the wooden bowl of fruit on the table. She got out the milk and four glasses. They sat at the table talking, eating, and laughing.

Dad walked in, his car keys in his hand. "Hi ya, girls." He took a cookie. "I just got back from Kesha's place."

Chelsea leaped up. "What? Why didn't you take me with you?"

The others shot questions at Chelsea's dad too. He laughed as he pulled up a chair and sat down. He finished his cookie and took a drink of Chelsea's milk.

"Dad, tell us!" Chelsea locked her icy hands in her lap and tried to steady the wild beat of her heart.

"Kesha was there with two younger brothers. Her parents weren't there and never came while I was there. Kesha said they'd be home later, but I wondered . . ."

"What?" all the girls asked at once.

". . . whether they would be. There's something funny going on." He fingered his mustache. "But I don't know what. Maybe the Bronskis were going to be back. Then again, maybe not."

"What did her place look like?"

"An apartment that was too small for the whole family. Kesha was embarrassed that it looked so messy . . . and that I was there."

"I wish I could've gone with you," Chelsea said.

"I thought about that, but you had company."

"We all could've gone," Kathy said.

Hannah shook her head. "It might've scared her to have us all show up."

"I'd be scared." Kathy giggled.

Chelsea turned to Dad. "Did she ask about me?"

Dad nodded. "I told her you were all right."

"Good. She was worried."

Later after the Best Friends went home Chelsea sat in her room reading her Bible, and the words jumped right off the page and into her heart. She was a child of God—a new creation!

The phone rang, and she jumped. She waited, listening at her door in case Dad shouted to tell her it was for her. It was probably for Mom.

"Phone, Chel!" Dad called up the stairs.

"Thanks, Dad!" She scooped up the receiver. "Hello."

"It's me, Chel Sea."

"Kesha!" Chelsea sank to her chair.

"Your dad was here."

"I know."

"He's nice. He dresses nice and talks nice."

"Thanks."

"Not like my dad."

Chelsea stiffened. "Oh?"

"He yells, and he swears too."

"How about your mom?" Chelsea waited, barely breathing.

"Can I trust you, Chel?"

"Yes."

Kesha took a deep breath. "My mom's in the hospital . . . Well, not exactly a hospital. She drinks, so Dad took her to a place to dry out."

Chelsea leaned back, her eyes wide. She couldn't imagine Mom drinking or having to go to a hospital so she could stop drinking. How awful for Kesha! "How long has she been gone?"

Kesha was quiet a long time. "A week."

"I'm sure sorry, Kesha."

"Yeah, me too." Kesha laughed a tiny laugh. "But she'll be all right when she comes back. It'll be easier when she doesn't drink, Dad says."

Chelsea leaned forward, the receiver tight against her ear. "Are you making this story up, Kesha?"

"No!"

"Honest?"

"Cross my heart! I wouldn't make up stories to you. We're friends."

"You're right." And Chelsea meant it. They were friends, strange as it seemed. "I'll see you tomorrow."

"In the morning?"

"Sure. Come here early, and I'll let you wear something of mine if you want."

"You will? Thanks! But what about your mom and dad? They might not want me around you."

"They care about you, Kesha."

"They don't even know me!"

"We prayed for you. We want you to know Jesus loves you and wants to be your true friend."

"Thanks, Chel. See you in the morning."

"Okay." Chelsea twisted the phone cord around her finger. "Kesha, I'm sorry about you getting detention."

"It's nothing."

"But it is! The teachers won't trust you, and the students will always think the worst of you."

"I never thought about that."

"We'll have to change their minds."

"How?"

"By following the rules from now on and by not making trouble."

"I hope that works."

"Me too."

"Chel?"

"Yes?"

"Does Jesus really love me?"

"Yes. Want me to read a verse from the Bible for you?"

"Okay."

Chelsea turned the pages until she found John 3:16. "Kesha, 'for God so loved the world He gave his only Son Jesus; that whosoever believes in Him should not perish but should have everlasting life.'" Chelsea closed her Bible. "Jesus died for you."

"I heard about that on TV, but I didn't know if it was true."

"It is. Jesus didn't stay dead—He rose again. He

111

lives in Heaven now, and He prays for you and me. He does love you, Kesha. He really does want to be your personal friend and your personal Savior."

Kesha sniffed. Was she crying? "Thanks, Chel. See you in the morning."

"See ya." Chelsea slowly hung up. She lifted her face and whispered, "Jesus, let Kesha know You really do love her."

11

The Missing Camera

Chelsea stood aside as Kesha rummaged through the closet. Kesha's blonde curls bounced on her shoulders. She was wearing the lime-green and orange outfit she'd worn Monday. The clothes she'd borrowed from Chelsea were neatly folded on Chelsea's bed. Chelsea leaned against her desk. She'd already shown Kesha the things Mom had said she absolutely couldn't borrow.

Shaking her head, Kesha turned away from the rack of clothes. "I can't choose! There's too much to choose from!"

"I'll do it for you." Chelsea picked a denim skirt and an orange-and-red top. "You can leave on your orange tights." She held the outfit up to Kesha. "It looks great, don't you think?"

Kesha frowned slightly. "But you're wearing dress pants. Shouldn't I too?"

"It doesn't matter." Just then Chelsea noticed a hole in Kesha's tights.

"I never wore a skirt before." Kesha looked it over. "But if you say it'll look good, I'll wear it."

"Wait . . . Jeans would be better to cover up that hole."

Kesha looked behind her knee where Chelsea was pointing. "Oh no! This is the only pair of tights I have that still looks good."

Chelsea shrugged. "Just wear jeans, and nobody will see the holes."

Kesha sank to the edge of the bed. "Chel, I can't keep borrowing clothes from you, but all of mine are worn-out."

"Don't think about it now, Kesha. We have to hurry to catch the bus." Chelsea handed Kesha a pair of jeans to wear with the top she'd chosen. "Want a banana to eat on the way to the bus?"

"Sure! Thanks."

Chelsea wanted to ask Kesha if she had enough food at her house, but she didn't want to embarrass her.

Several minutes later in the bright morning sunlight Chelsea walked with Kesha toward the bus. A robin sang from the top of a maple. Just as Kesha finished her banana, Hannah and Roxie joined them. They all said hi to each other, then walked along in silence. Hannah's little sisters ran on ahead. Their laughter floated back.

"We're really sorry you have detention," Roxie finally said.

Kesha shrugged. "It's not so bad."

Chelsea frantically searched her mind for something to say. "I hope we don't have another quiz in science today."

"I like science," Hannah and Kesha said together. They looked at each other and giggled, then started talking about what they liked best about it. They sat together on the bus and continued talking.

Chelsea, with Roxie beside her, sat just in back of Hannah and Kesha. The bus smelled like a tuna sandwich and dirty socks put together.

Roxie leaned close to Chelsea and whispered, "Kesha's not as bad as I thought."

"I know." Chelsea smiled. She was glad Roxie felt that way. It would be hard to have Kesha as a friend if the Best Friends didn't like or trust her.

At school Chelsea hurried to her homeroom with Kesha and the Best Friends beside her. Chelsea thought she heard someone whisper her name and saw someone point at her, but she was afraid to look.

In the classroom she sank to her desk and opened her reading book. Whispers buzzed all around her. What was going on? She glanced around and found several students looking at her. They looked quickly away, and she flushed. She turned to Kesha and whispered, "What's going on?"

Kesha spread her hands and grinned. "I guess they all know who we are now. We aren't invisible any longer."

Chelsea wished she was. Being stared at and talked about was awful!

Just then the intercom crackled, and a voice said, "Chelsea McCrea and Kesha Bronski, report to the principal's office immediately."

Chelsea sank low and groaned.

Kesha jumped right up. "Come on, Chel! It's another great adventure."

Chelsea hung her head as she followed Kesha from the room. This was worse than before. What gossip would the students spread this time?

Kesha tossed her head and laughed as they hurried down the empty hall. "Maybe they want to tell us we no longer have detention."

Chelsea scowled at her. "Oh, sure."

"Maybe your dad called and said to get us off detention."

"No way. I wanted him to, but he wouldn't. He said we have to serve our time for doing wrong."

Kesha's face fell. "Oh. Then why are we being called?"

"I don't know." Chelsea's voice broke. Being called to the office twice in one week was totally embarrassing.

"Well, whatever it is, we can handle it without any problem." Kesha ran ahead and walked right into the office and up to the desk. The woman sitting there continued to write in a ledger.

Her skin on fire, Chelsea hung back while Kesha announced they were there.

The woman looked up with a scowl. "Mrs. Evans is expecting you. Go right in."

Kesha walked to the door, waited a split second, then opened it. "Good morning, Mrs. Evans."

Chelsea slipped in quietly without making a sound. She was afraid that if she tried to talk she'd burst into wild tears.

Mrs. Evans looked very stern. "Sit down, girls. This is very serious business." She fingered her red beads and then touched her matching red earrings. She wore a navy-blue suit with a red-and-white blouse.

Chelsea's legs gave way, and she dropped into the gold plastic chair. She clung to the arms of the chair so tightly her knuckles turned white.

Kesha crossed her legs and rested her hands in her lap. For once she didn't speak.

Mrs. Evans tapped a yellow pencil on her notebook. "I haven't called your parents yet." She narrowed her eyes as she looked at Kesha. "Did you bring a note from your parents?"

Kesha shook her head. "My dad read your note, but he was too tired to answer it. He said he'd call you or something."

"Fine." Mrs. Evans tapped the pencil again. "Girls, yesterday a camera was stolen from the eighth grade photography class."

Chelsea shivered.

"That's terrible!" Kesha clicked her tongue. "Really awful!"

"It was the Nikon N2000 that you both looked at and talked about when you invaded the class."

Chelsea's stomach turned over, and a bitter taste

117

filled her mouth just like when she was about to throw up.

"I hope you find out who took it," Kesha said sharply. "That was a nice camera."

Mrs. Evans cleared her throat. "Two girls saw you two near that classroom yesterday after your P.E. class."

"The gym is near the class." Kesha leaned forward. "We had to be near the room since we were in gym."

"The girls said they saw you slip out of the classroom . . . And they were sure you had the camera with you."

Chelsea gasped.

"Never!" Kesha leaped up. "We didn't take the camera! Honest!"

"Not even to use?" Mrs. Evans slowly stood. "I think you wanted to use it, so you borrowed it, and you haven't been able to return it."

"No way!" Kesha jerked Chelsea up. "Tell her! We didn't do it!"

"We didn't," Chelsea whispered weakly.

Mrs. Evans pointed her pencil at Chelsea. "You don't sound very sure."

"She's scared!" Kesha slipped her arm around Chelsea's waist. "She's not used to being called to the principal's office."

"Yet she's been here twice in such a short time," Mrs. Evans said dryly.

Kesha patted Chelsea's arm. "Are you okay?"

Chelsea shook her head.

"Sit back down, girls." Mrs. Evans sat again.

Chelsea dropped into her chair, and Kesha perched on the edge of hers.

"If you girls do have the camera, please return it immediately."

"We don't have it," Kesha said.

"We don't," Chelsea whispered hoarsely.

"We'll search your lockers, of course. And we'll be asking around the school to see if anyone else saw you in the photography room or with the camera." Mrs. Evans talked for a while about the importance of integrity and honestly. Finally she stood. The smell of a sweet cologne drifted out from her. "We'll look in your lockers now."

Kesha jumped up. "You won't find anything."

Chelsea stood, then almost collapsed again. She forced strength into her legs and slowly followed Kesha from the room. Mrs. Evans was behind her.

At her locker Chelsea fumbled with the combination but finally opened the door. It clattered back against the locker beside it, and she jumped nervously. She felt so guilty, she almost expected to see the camera sitting inside. But it wasn't. Only two books and a notebook sat there.

Mrs. Evans peered on the shelf behind the books, then stepped back. "You may close it."

Chelsea pushed it shut, and the bang sounded especially loud in the silent hall.

"My locker's near the water fountain." Kesha ran

ahead and quickly opened it. She lifted her chin and stepped to the side.

Mrs. Evans looked in Kesha's locker, then asked her to close it. "You girls may go back to class." She held a pass out to Kesha. "If you have the camera, please return it." She walked away without a backward glance.

Kesha wadded up the pass and tossed it to the scuff-marked floor. "I won't go back to class!"

"But we have to!" Chelsea picked up the note and smoothed it out.

"How can anybody think we took that camera? We didn't."

"Skipping class won't help at all."

Kesha nodded and laughed. "You're right! We're innocent. Everybody will believe us."

"I hope so . . . if they don't think we're guilty because of what we did already."

"We're innocent, so we'll act innocent."

Chelsea peeked at Kesha from under her long lashes. Was Kesha really innocent?

Kesha grabbed the pass. "Let's get into class. We sure don't want Mr. Borgman to think we're skipping." Kesha squeezed Chelsea's arm. "I'm right here with you, Chel."

"Thanks." Just then Chelsea remembered that God was with her too. Silently she prayed someone would find the camera and prove she and Kesha weren't guilty.

In the homeroom Mr. Borgman was having a discussion on a story they'd just read. Kesha handed him the pass, and he nodded, then dropped it to his desk.

With a million eyes on her, Chelsea sank to her seat, and Kesha sat beside her. The room smelled stuffy and felt hot.

Mr. Borgman asked a question, and a girl answered. Everyone laughed, but Chelsea couldn't understand why.

Toward the end of class she felt a poke in her back. She glanced over her shoulder, and the boy behind her pushed a note at her. She didn't want to take it but did anyway. It burned a hole in her hand, but she wouldn't open it right now. Mr. Borgman might see. She wanted to toss the note in the wastebasket, but she couldn't without reading it first. She just had to know what it said!

After class she hurried into the hall and stood with her back pressed to the wall to leave room for the students to rush on past.

Kesha hurried to Chelsea's side. "What's wrong?"

"Someone gave me a note."

"You better let me read it. It might hurt you too much." Kesha took it and opened it. She glanced over it, then balled it up. Her face turned red. "It's got bad words in it. You don't want to read it."

Chelsea trembled. "Why would anyone write a note like that to me?"

"Somebody thinks you took the camera."

"But I didn't! I couldn't do such a terrible thing!"

Just then the Best Friends walked up and asked Chelsea what was wrong. Kesha told them about the stolen camera and the note.

"That's terrible!" Hannah looked ready to cry.

"We don't have time to talk about it now," Kathy said. "We have to get to math before we're all tardy."

"We sure don't want any more things against us!" Kesha hurried toward math class with Roxie and Hannah beside her.

Kathy caught Chelsea's arm. "Wait."

Chelsea looked questioningly at Kathy.

"How do you know Kesha didn't take the camera?"

"I just know!"

Kathy shook her head. "No. You want to believe her, so you do. She could've done it, Chel. Look at all the other things she did."

"Oh, Kathy, don't! . . . Please." Chelsea hugged her books to her. "I'm almost positive Kesha is innocent."

"I'm going to do what I can to find that camera. So will Hannah and Roxie."

"Thanks." Chelsea blinked back her tears.

Later, on the way to the cafeteria, Chelsea caught a glimpse of a notice on the bulletin board. "Wait, Kesha." Chelsea stopped and read the notice about Photography Club. All the students in the middle school were invited to join. They were to sign up in the photography classroom before the end of the day.

"We can sign up right now, then come back for lunch."

"Let's go! I'm starved, but I can wait a little longer."

Again Chelsea wanted to ask if they had enough food at their house, but she didn't.

A few minutes later Chelsea led the way into the classroom. Mr. Scott sat at his desk. He looked up with a frown.

"We came to sign up for Photography Club," Chelsea said, smiling.

"We're really excited about it." Kesha nodded and giggled.

Mr. Scott slowly stood. "You can sign up, but you can't participate until you're cleared of all charges of theft."

Chelsea's heart zoomed to her feet. "But we didn't take the camera. Honest!"

"We sure didn't." Kesha bent over the paper and signed her name with a flare. "And we'll prove it!"

Chelsea's hand shook as she signed her name. She lifted her head and looked Mr. Scott straight in the eye. "We would never steal."

"Never!" Kesha tossed her head and marched out.

In the hall Chelsea's eyes filled with tears. "It's terrible to be suspected of stealing." She remembered when she'd worked for Mrs. Sobol when she'd first started *King's Kids*. Mrs. Sobol had actually accused her of stealing her dune buggy right out of her garage!

Chelsea brushed at her tears. She hadn't stolen the dune buggy then, and she hadn't stolen the camera now. She had to convince Mr. Scott and the others that she was innocent.

"We're not guilty, so we don't have anything to worry about." Kesha smiled as she tugged on Chelsea's arm. "We got to get to lunch before it's too late for us to eat. We still have detention, you know."

Shivers ran down Chelsea's spine as she hurried to the cafeteria with Kesha. Another day of detention! Would this week ever end?

12

A Talk with the Teachers

Trembling, Chelsea stepped into detention. Gina, Lucile, and Tilly were already there talking to the two boys. They all grew very quiet and stared at her, and then Lucile snickered behind her hand. They all looked toward the blackboard. Chelsea did too. She gasped. Her name was written on the blackboard with dirty words all around it.

Kesha dashed to the board and erased it. She turned and glared at the girls. "Don't do that again!"

"She stole a camera," Gina said, pointing at Chelsea.

"I did not!"

"She did not," Kesha snapped.

"You both took it! We know. We saw you!" Gina shook her finger at Chelsea and Kesha. "We told!"

"So it was you!" Kesha stamped her foot. "I should've known."

"What's all the yelling about?" Mr. Murphy asked as he walked in and headed for his desk.

"They said we stole a camera, but we didn't." Kesha marched right up to Mr. Murphy's desk. "They probably took it just to make trouble for us."

"We did not!"

"Sit down, Kesha. Now!" Mr. Murphy frowned at the others. "All of you, get your work sheets and start working on them. I don't want to hear another sound. Got it?"

Chelsea waited until the others picked up their work sheets, and then she slowly walked to Mr. Murphy's desk. She cleared her throat.

He frowned at her. "Yes?"

She shivered and locked her legs to keep from falling. In a low voice she said, "We didn't take the camera. We really didn't. How can we convince the teachers of that?"

Mr. Murphy studied Chelsea for a long time. "I understand this is your first time in detention."

She nodded.

"Here in Michigan? How about in Oklahoma?"

Chelsea's eyes widened. "Never in Oklahoma! I never got in trouble."

"If that's true, then you should be able to convince the teachers of your innocence."

"But how?"

"Call a meeting with them. Ask Mrs. Evans to let you do that. You have a right to be heard."

Chelsea smiled in relief. "Thank you! I'll do it!"

"Your little friend Kesha might not be as fortunate. She has caused trouble in every school she's ever attended."

"But that was before she started hanging out with me. She won't any longer."

Mr. Murphy frowned. "I'll give her the benefit of the doubt. But you should be on your guard. It's very hard for someone to change."

"She's got help." Chelsea smiled.

"Maybe there is hope for her." Mr. Murphy tapped his pencil impatiently. "Sit down and get to work before the time is up."

"Thank you!" Chelsea hurried to her seat. She glanced across the room in time to catch Tilly glaring at her. She shivered as she sat down. What had she done to make the three girls so angry at her? Kesha had warned her not to act like a snob. Maybe they thought she had.

Chelsea read over the questions and answered as many as she could. She skipped the questions about Earth and stars. How was she supposed to remember all those details? The last question made her smile. *What does friendship mean to you?* She could answer that easily. She bent over her paper and wrote:

When I lived in Oklahoma I had a best friend, Sidney. We lived next door to each other all our lives. When my dad got transferred to Grand Rapids, we had to move to Middle Lake, Michigan. I had to leave Sidney. It hurt a lot. I cried because I missed her so much. I even called her on the phone and ran up a terrible bill that I had to pay for myself. So I started the *King's Kids*. It's a group of kids who want to do odd jobs to make money. I'm the president. So while I worked I got to know other kids. I met the Ottawa Indian girl, Hannah, who lived across the street from me. She was really really nice. I also met Roxie, the girl right next door to me. I didn't like her much at first. But I learned to love her. And then I met Kathy in the park. We all started talking together and working together. Soon we were Best Friends. We started a Best Friends Club. We agreed to do good deeds for others and to have fun together and share secrets with each other. We read a Bible verse together each day we meet. We all have Jesus as our very Best Friend. He is our King too. One day I met Kesha Bronski. She was different than my other friends. She skipped class and she made up stories. But she didn't know these things were wrong to do. She thought she could do them because it made her and me happy. But that got us both in trouble. But Kesha is my friend even if she isn't perfect. I'm not perfect either. I want to help Kesha learn you can't do things to make yourself happy. You have to think about your actions, and if they're wrong, don't do them. I think she'll learn. I let a new friend into my life, a friend who isn't always perfect, but she's a friend anyway— Kesha Bronski. It's important to be friendly and to have friends.

Just as Chelsea finished, the bell rang. She handed in her paper. She noticed that Mr. Murphy picked it up before the others could put theirs on top of it. Was he going to grade hers first? She wanted to ask, but Kesha nudged her to hurry out of the room.

In the hall Chelsea caught Kesha's arm and hurried her toward the office. Silently Chelsea prayed for the right words to say to Mrs. Evans.

"Hey, where are we going?" Kesha pulled back, but Chelsea wouldn't let her go.

"Mr. Murphy told me to ask for a meeting with the teachers so we can convince them we didn't steal the camera."

"Ha! You think they'll listen to me?" Kesha looked down at herself, then giggled. "Hey, they might. I have on your clothes today, and I'm with you."

Chelsea walked right into the office to the woman behind the desk. "I need to see Mrs. Evans right away please."

"She's busy."

"It's urgent."

"It is," Kesha said, grinning.

The woman picked up the phone and spoke to

Mrs. Evans. She hung up and said, "She has a few minutes. Go on in."

Chelsea took a deep breath and walked into Mrs. Evans's office. It smelled like roses.

Mrs. Evans looked up from a paper she was reading. "What can I do for you girls?"

Chelsea wanted to run from the office, but she squared her shoulders and looked right at Mrs. Evans. "We did not steal or borrow the camera. We want to tell the teachers that and make them believe us. Could you call a meeting so we can talk?"

Kesha giggled nervously.

Mrs. Evans sighed heavily. "I find it very hard to believe you. Because I don't know either of you, nor do the other teachers, I find it hard to believe you didn't take the camera. Your actions speak more loudly than your words."

Chelsea nodded. "My dad always says that. But most of my actions are good ones."

"She was only following me when she got in trouble." Kesha lifted her chin. "But we didn't steal the camera. We skipped class and went where we shouldn't have, but that's not stealing."

Mrs. Evans nodded. "You're right. It's not stealing." She looked down at her paper. "There's a teachers' meeting just before the close of school. You may both attend and have your say."

"Thank you!" Chelsea breathed a sigh of relief.

Kesha moved closer to the desk. "Could you give us a pass to leave social studies early?"

Mrs. Evans nodded. She dashed out a note and handed it to Kesha. "See you later."

"For sure." Kesha smiled, then turned to Chelsea. "You've got more nerve than I thought."

"We have to clear our names." Chelsea smiled at Mrs. Evans. "I guess we'll need a pass to get into English since we'll get there late."

"I'm getting writer's cramp just supplying you with passes." Mrs. Evans wrote out another one and handed it to Chelsea. "Hurry to class now."

"We will." Chelsea rushed out of the office with Kesha close beside her.

"How come it's so important to clear our names?" Kesha asked as they sped down the empty hall toward English class.

"Because we don't want to have a bad reputation. I belong to Jesus, and that means I'm His ambassador. If I have a bad name, so does He."

"I never thought of that."

"Now that you have, you do want your name cleared, don't you?"

"Sure I do!"

"Good." Chelsea smiled, then opened the door and walked into English class. She caught the questioning looks of the Best Friends and smiled reassuringly, then hurried to hand the note to Mr. Borgman.

After class the Best Friends crowded around Chelsea and Kesha to find out why they'd been late to class. As quickly as she could, Chelsea explained.

"In case I miss the bus, tell my mom and she'll pick me up. And Kesha too."

Hannah nodded.

"We have to get to P.E. fast!" Chelsea rushed down the hall toward the stairs with the girls beside her. Once they got to P.E., the class seemed to drag. And later, in social studies, Chelsea looked at her watch every few minutes. At long last it was time to leave. Kesha had already given Mr. Borgman the pass to leave early. He'd left five minutes before. A sub was taking care of the class until the end of the school day.

In the hall Kesha took a deep breath. "I'm usually never scared, but I am today." She dropped a book. It echoed throughout the empty hall. "I'm leaving the books at my locker."

"I'll put mine in with yours to save time." Chelsea hurried to Kesha's locker with her.

Kesha fumbled with the combination. "I really am nervous," she said with a giggle.

Just then a man in a dark suit strode down the hall. He frowned at the girls. "Do you have permission to be in the hall?" he asked sharply.

Kesha nodded and dropped her books.

The man bent to pick them up.

"We're on our way to a meeting." Chelsea's mouth suddenly felt bone-dry.

Kesha finally swung her locker open. The man stuck her books on the shelf and stepped back. Chelsea put hers on the locker floor, and Kesha shut the door with a bang. The man hurried away.

Chelsea breathed a sigh of relief as she and Kesha rushed down the hall. To her surprise the man went in the same room they were going to.

"I hope he doesn't say something bad about me for dropping my books," Kesha whispered.

Chelsea shivered as she opened the door and walked in. Mrs. Evans stood at the front of the room. The teachers sat around a big table. The man from the hall sat nearest to Mrs. Evans.

"Come in, girls," Mrs. Evans said crisply. "We've been expecting you. You may come right up here and say what you want to say."

The room spun. Chelsea closed her eyes. Deep inside she heard a soft voice say, "I'm always with you, Chelsea." She smiled and lifted her head high.

Mrs. Evans sat down as the girls walked to the front of the room.

Her mouth dry, Chelsea stood beside Kesha and looked at the teachers staring back at her. She saw Mr. Murphy from detention and flushed with embarrassment.

"Go right ahead, Chelsea," Mrs. Evans said.

"I am new at this school. So is Kesha. So we hung around together. Kesha was trying to help me survive in a new school. We left class because of a lie, and we went where we weren't supposed to, but we did not steal the camera. You can call my old school to see what kind of girl I am. I never ever even got called to the principal's office. And I never had detention in my entire life until this week. I don't steal, and I never will!" Chelsea turned to Kesha. "Do you want to say anything?"

Kesha grinned. "I have been to detention a lot and to the principal's office a lot. Not in this school, of course. But I never got sent for stealing anything. I was only trying to make myself happy. If a class didn't make me happy, I left. I don't steal, and I never will." She smiled at Chelsea. "Right, Chel Sea?"

"Right."

Mr. Murphy slowly stood. "Mrs. Evans, with your permission I'd like to read something Chelsea wrote."

"Do so."

Chelsea bit her lip. What was he going to read?

Mr. Murphy read the paragraphs Chelsea had written in detention—the one telling why she'd never be in detention again, and also what she'd written about friends.

Chelsea moved restlessly. It was embarrassing to hear her own words read aloud for all the teachers to hear.

When he finished he said, "Now for Kesha's." He shuffled his papers a bit. "'I hope to never be in detention again. But I don't know how to stay out. I think Chelsea will teach me. She knows a lot about being a good girl. I teased her about always obeying, but she's right. It is better to obey. If I can learn to do that, I won't be in detention again.'"

Chelsea smiled at Kesha.

"It's true," Kesha said, grinning.

"Here's Kesha's paragraph on friends." Mr. Murphy cleared his throat. "'I never in my whole life had a friend before. We move all the time, and I go to a new school every year. I meet lots of kids and get to know them, but I never got to be friends with any of them. Chelsea is my friend. She even let me be friends with her three best friends. I think that's nice. She let me borrow her clothes, and she gave me a banana when I was really really hungry. She said she's going to tell me all about Jesus so He can be my very Best Friend. No matter where we move next I'd always have Jesus, my very Best Friend, with me.'" Mr. Murphy looked at the teachers and then at Mrs. Evans. "I for one choose to believe these girls. They didn't take the camera."

Chelsea's heart leaped. Then she saw the looks on a few of the teachers' faces. They still weren't convinced.

Kesha squeezed Chelsea's arm and whispered, "Don't give up."

Chelsea lifted her chin high. She wouldn't give up. She wasn't guilty! And neither was Kesha!

Just then a boy burst into the room. "We found the camera!"

"Where?" Mrs. Evans asked sharply.

Chelsea smiled in relief at Kesha.

The boy looked at the teachers and then right at Kesha. "In Kesha Bronski's locker."

Chelsea gasped. Kesha's face turned ashen. She shook her head helplessly.

Chelsea caught Kesha's hand and held on tight.

13

The Campaign

As all the teachers were staring at them, Chelsea felt Kesha tremble. "We know it's a lie," Chelsea whispered.

"But they think it's the truth!" Kesha motioned toward the teachers.

Looking very stern, Mrs. Evans cleared her throat. "Bring the camera here to me." She looked right at the girls. "The truth at last! So much for all your fine talk."

The boy set the camera on the table and started back to the door.

"Hold it!" The man in the dark suit stood to his feet.

"What is it, Mr. Ekland?" Mrs. Evans asked with a slight smile.

"He's the school superintendent," Kesha whispered in awe.

"Come back up here, young man." Mr. Ekland waved his hand.

The boy slowly returned to the front of the room. His face was brick-red, and he looked like he wanted to run away.

"What's your name?" Mr. Ekland asked kindly.

"Sam Jennings."

Mr. Ekland rested his hand on the boy's shoulder. "Sam, tell us exactly where you found the camera."

Sam swallowed hard.

"Take your time," Mrs. Evans said stiffly.

Sam nervously rubbed his hands down his jeans. "The dismissal bell just rang, and I was in the hall at my locker. It's right beside Kesha's. A guy bumped against her locker, then jerked it open. I saw the camera inside. The guy said the teachers were all meeting here. He gave me the camera, so I brought it."

"Now are you satisfied?" Mrs. Evans asked as she scowled at Mr. Ekland.

He shook his head. "Come here, girls."

Chelsea and Kesha slowly walked over to him. He smiled down at them, then turned to the others and told about seeing them in the hall just before the meeting.

"Kesha dropped her books, and I picked them up and put them in her locker myself. Chelsea put hers in, and Kesha closed the door. I saw no camera. All three of us came to the meeting, and we've all three been here ever since." Mr. Ekland studied the teachers and Mrs. Evans. "You might ask, how did the camera get in Kesha's locker? Someone put it there to frame her."

The teachers gasped and whispered.

"The girls are innocent." Mr. Ekland stood silently for a while. "We accused them of stealing, but we were wrong." He looked at Chelsea and Kesha. "We are sorry for what we did. From what I've heard at this meeting I know you're both sorry for the things you did that put you in detention. I suspend your detention. You no longer have to go. That's my way of saying we're sorry for putting you through the agony of being accused of stealing." He turned to Mrs. Evans. "Do you agree?"

"Of course! Girls, we are all sorry. We'll learn the truth about the camera." Her face ashen, Mrs. Evans turned to Sam. "Who discovered the camera in Kesha's locker?"

"Ben Bartell."

Mr. Murphy stood. "Ben has detention for the rest of the month. He and some of the others in detention have tried to make trouble for Chelsea."

Mrs. Evans's eyes flashed. "We'll speak to Ben Bartell in the morning."

Mr. Ekland tapped Chelsea's shoulder. "You girls get to your bus before it leaves you behind."

"Thanks." Chelsea smiled at everyone in the room. "Thank you all for listening to us."

"Thanks." Kesha giggled. "We're sure glad we're out of trouble."

Chelsea tugged Kesha across the room and out the door. They looked at each other and laughed. Suddenly the smile died on Kesha's face.

"What?" Chelsea asked as they ran outdoors for the bus.

"Somebody hates me enough to frame me for stealing the camera. Who would it be? Ben? Gina? Lucile? Tilly?"

"We'll find out. Or maybe it doesn't even matter. Maybe we just need to be thankful that our names have been cleared and just keep ourselves out of trouble from here on." Chelsea stopped beside her bus. "Are you riding home with me?"

Kesha giggled. "Sure, but I don't have permission."

Chelsea helplessly shook her head as she found a seat to share with Kesha.

Later at home Chelsea and Kesha sat in the kitchen eating cheese and crackers and drinking apple juice. Chelsea told Mom and the boys what had happened. A few minutes later the Best Friends came over, and the girls sat in the backyard and told their story again.

Hannah burst out laughing. "I have the best idea in the whole entire world!"

"What?"

"Start a campaign to tell everyone that the girls didn't steal the camera and that they're nice."

"Good!" Kathy nodded excitedly. "We'll do it!"

"I'll make a flyer and pass it out all over school." Roxie locked her arms around her knees and rocked back and forth on the picnic table.

Just then Mom called Chelsea to the phone. She excused herself and ran inside to the kitchen phone.

Breathlessly she said, "Hello. This is Chelsea McCrea."

"This is Margot Murphy. I understand you do odd jobs."

"That's right." Chelsea grabbed the pencil and pad she kept by each phone for that very reason. "I'll need your name, address, phone number, and the job you need done."

The woman gave her address and phone number. "I need my spare bedroom cleaned. It's been a junk room for the last three years, but now I need it for a bedroom. How soon can you come?"

"I'll call you back right away. Thank you for calling." Chelsea hung up, then quickly dialed Hannah's mom. She knew a lot of people in the area. When Hannah's mom answered, Chelsea gave her the details.

"I think Margot Murphy is a teacher's wife. Let me make a call and I'll get right back to you."

"Thanks, Mrs. Shigwam." Chelsea hung up, then shouted out the back door to tell the girls what she was waiting for. "You girls can come inside to wait with me if you want."

They ran in as Kesha asked all about the *King's Kids*. She wanted to join, but she lived too far away.

"But you could start *King's Kids* in your area," Chelsea said. "You could be the president. But be sure to check out every person who calls in. It's not safe to go to a stranger's house."

Roxie asked for paper and markers and started to work on a flyer. The others crowded around her as she sketched Chelsea and Kesha on the paper.

The phone rang, and Chelsea leaped to answer it. Mrs. Shigwam took a deep breath. "Margot Murphy is not Mr. Murphy's wife but his mother. She lives just outside The Ravines, and she's a fine woman. You can safely go work for her."

"Thank you." Chelsea hung up and quickly dialed Mrs. Murphy back. When Mrs. Murphy answered, Chelsea told her when she could work and how much money she expected. "I'd like to have someone come help me because during the school year we don't work as many hours as during the summer."

"That'll be fine. I'll expect you tomorrow at 4."

"We'll be there. Thanks for calling." Chelsea hung up and told the others who Mrs. Murphy was. "I wonder if Mr. Murphy from school told her about the *King's Kids*."

Kesha ran to Chelsea and caught her arm. "I'd like to help you tomorrow. Can I?"

"I don't know. Would your dad let you?"

"Sure. He never cares where I am."

Chelsea felt bad for Kesha, but she didn't say so. "Then I guess you can."

"Good!" Kesha sighed. "I've got to get home now." She'd changed from Chelsea's clothes earlier. "See you in the morning."

"See ya." Chelsea grabbed an apple and tossed it

to Kesha. "Here's something to eat on your way home."

"Thanks." Kesha grinned and then slipped out the door.

Roxie held up a flyer. "Look!" She'd already drawn a picture of Kesha and Chelsea dressed in their brightly colored clothes. She'd written, "They're bright. They're beautiful. They're honest. They did not steal the camera. Everyone knows that."

"Nice work." Chelsea pointed to her picture and giggled. "I can't believe I really dressed like that."

"You sure did!" Kathy playfully tugged Chelsea's hair.

A few minutes later the Best Friends went home, and Chelsea did her math homework and the usual chores. She thought about the day she'd had and smiled. "Thank You, Jesus, for always being with me and for helping me." She couldn't wait to tell Dad everything. He'd be glad.

The next afternoon at school Chelsea walked into English class with Kesha. Chelsea had looked for the Best Friends after she'd gone to her locker but couldn't find them. But she knew they'd be around soon. They were her friends.

Chelsea opened her English book. This was a whole new day! She didn't have detention any longer, and she wasn't new in school. But best of all, she could participate in Photography Club. She'd even heard there was going to be a contest, and the best photo would win money toward a camera. Maybe she'd win.

Just then someone tossed a tightly folded note to Chelsea. It landed with a plop on her book. Class hadn't started yet, so she opened it. It was a flyer that Roxie had put up on the bulletin board, but someone had scribbled out some words and added others. It read: "They're dull. They're ugly. They're dishonest. And they did steal the camera."

Chelsea wadded up the flyer, but before she could throw it away Kesha grabbed it and smoothed it out so she could read it.

Kesha's cheeks turned red, and her eyes snapped with anger. "I thought nobody would say these things after yesterday."

"Don't let it upset you," Chelsea whispered. "You know the truth."

Kesha helplessly shook her head. "I'm out of here." She jumped up and ran from the room.

Chelsea hesitated a second, then sped after Kesha. She caught up with her in the hallway. She gripped her arm and wouldn't let her pull away. "You have to go back in, Kesha! You can't skip class!"

"I can do anything I want!" Kesha tried to pry Chelsea's fingers loose. "I don't want to feel this way. Let me do what makes me happy!"

Chelsea shook her head. "It doesn't really make you happy, Kesha. You can put the problem out of your mind, but the problem is still there. Let's go back into class before the tardy bell rings. Please!"

Kesha's eyes filled with tears. "Don't bother with me, Chel. I'm not worth it."

Chelsea giggled. "Don't give me that, Kesha. You know you are! Besides, I happen to know that God made you in His image and that you are valuable to Him."

Kesha brushed at her tears. "I never met anybody like you before."

"I know." Chelsea giggled, and finally Kesha joined in. They hurried back into class and sat down just as the tardy bell rang.

It seemed to Chelsea that the day zipped past. The flyers made some people happy and others angry. Many of the students stopped Chelsea to tell her they believed her.

During social studies the intercom crackled, and then Mrs. Evans announced, "We have found the person who stole the camera. It's back where it belongs. The student will continue in detention. I want all of you to know Chelsea McCrea and Kesha Bronski are not guilty, nor were they ever guilty."

"Hoorah!" Kathy shouted as she clapped. Others joined in, and Chelsea laughed right out loud. Kesha finally did too.

Mr. Borgman clapped along with them. He stood up and walked around to the front of his desk. "Boys and girls, many of us forgot that the law says we're innocent until proved guilty. Chelsea and Kesha insisted they were innocent, but many of us didn't believe them because of their actions before that.

They've apologized for their actions and have agreed to follow all the rules after this." He smiled at the girls. "Now let's put this behind us and get back to social studies."

Grinning, Chelsea peeked at Kesha. She saw a sad look on Kesha's face but didn't understand it.

After school, on the way to work for Margot Murphy, Chelsea asked Kesha why she'd looked so sad after Mr. Borgman's speech.

"I don't think I can keep following all the rules, Chel! I mean, that's really really hard to do!"

"I'll help you. And Jesus will help you."

"How do I *know* that?"

"By *knowing* Jesus." Chelsea told Kesha about reading her Bible, praying, and going to church. "It's not really enough just to read the Bible. You have to obey what it says." Chelsea grinned. "You're getting good about obeying."

"Not really."

"Jesus will help you obey." Chelsea wanted to say more, but they reached Margot Murphy's house just then. Chelsea rang the doorbell.

"I'm glad I got to come with you."

"And you'll get paid. The *King's Kids* do good deeds where they don't charge, but this is a job we will be paid for."

Mrs. Murphy answered the door with a happy smile. She was short and plump with gray hair mixed with dark brown. She wore dark pants and a pink blouse.

"I'm Chelsea McCrea, and this is Kesha Bronski. She's going to help me."

"Kesha? I'm delighted to meet you. And you too, Chelsea. Come right in."

Kesha hesitated, but Chelsea urged her to go on in.

Her brown eyes sparkling, Mrs. Murphy told the girls what she wanted them to do as she led them to the bedroom. "The room isn't very big, but it's full of three years of stuff." She wrinkled her nose. "Or should I say junk?"

"We'll clean it for you." Chelsea picked up an empty box and started to fill it with newspapers.

"You girls can come to the kitchen for a snack in an hour." Mrs. Murphy smiled and walked away.

Helplessly, Kesha looked around. "How do you even know where to start?"

"Pick up that pile of clothes, fold them, and stack them away in boxes. Every little bit helps." Chelsea stuck more newspapers in the box. "Once we pick up the stuff just lying around, we'll be able to see what really needs to be done."

"I don't know if I could do this all the time."

"It does get hard, but it's nice to have extra money." Chelsea picked up a newspaper, startling a spider. She squealed, and it raced across the room.

Kesha stepped on it and said, "Yuk!"

Chelsea giggled. "We make a good team."

Kesha picked up a dress and folded it. "My dad

146

said my mom might not get to come home as soon as he thought."

"I'm sorry. We'll pray for her."

"Thanks."

Chelsea worked fast. Several times she had to tell Kesha what to do. The first job was usually the hardest. After an hour they washed up in the bathroom and then walked to the kitchen. The smell of pizza made Chelsea's mouth water.

"Sit down, girls." Mrs. Murphy set a pizza in the middle of the table and filled glasses with ice water.

"It smells great!" Kesha smiled at Mrs. Murphy. "It was really nice of you to fix it for us."

"I have kids of my own . . . all grown now . . . But I remember how hungry they'd get." Mrs. Murphy put a slice of pizza on the plates. "Tell me about yourselves while you eat."

Chelsea talked a while, then ate while Kesha talked. Before the pizza was finished they'd told Mrs. Murphy about the past few days. She listened with interest, asking questions at times.

Later Chelsea led Kesha back to the bedroom. "Now we'll dust and vacuum and make the bed with clean sheets."

Kesha dusted without speaking. Finally she turned to Chelsea. "I like Mrs. Murphy, but I think something's going on. She asked a lot of questions, didn't she?"

"Adults usually do that when you talk to them." Chelsea pulled clean sheets out of the closet. Was

Kesha right? Chelsea shivered. Maybe they shouldn't have told Mrs. Murphy so many things about school and their problems. But they'd told her the good things too.

"This is really a nice bedroom, but not as nice as yours, Chel. I wonder who's going to use it."

"Mrs. Murphy didn't say."

"I'll ask her."

"You don't want her to think you're nosy."

"She asked us a lot of questions."

Mrs. Murphy stuck her head in the door. "You girls did a marvelous job!"

"Thanks," they both said, then grinned at each other.

"I see you're almost done. Tell me when you finish, and I'll drive you both home. I'm sure you're tired after such a long day."

Chelsea *was* tired, but she didn't want to say so. She was thankful she wouldn't have to walk home.

Later when the bedroom was finished Kesha looked around and smiled. "It looks like a whole different room! We did a good job."

"Sure did." Tiredly Chelsea brushed a strand of her red hair back. A warm breeze blew in the two windows, airing out the room.

Kesha slowly walked over to Chelsea. "Something's going on, Chel. I can feel it."

"I don't know what it could be."

Kesha grinned. "Oh, it's probably just my imagination."

"I hope so. Can you come over Saturday afternoon? And go to church with us on Sunday?" Chelsea and the Best Friends were planning a special surprise party for Kesha on Saturday.

Kesha nodded.

"Good!"

Later Chelsea and Kesha climbed into Mrs. Murphy's car. She dropped Chelsea off first.

"Thanks for the ride, Mrs. Murphy."

"You're very welcome."

Chelsea waved good-bye to Kesha, then slowly walked to her house. Was something going on she should be concerned about? A shiver ran down her spine, and then she laughed. She was letting Kesha's imagination run away with her. Wasn't she?

14

A Made-over Kesha

Saturday Chelsea set the decorated cake on the counter in the basement. Red, blue, yellow, and green helium-filled balloons hung in clusters around the special rec room. The Best Friends had each brought something to eat or drink. They'd all wrapped the clothes they were giving Kesha in bright gift paper. Kesha hadn't seen the special rec room yet. She'd like it as much as everyone else did. She'd especially like the party and gifts they'd put together just for her.

"I hope she doesn't decide to stay home today." Hannah looked toward the stairs with a frown.

"Not Kesha." Kathy giggled. "She'd live here if she could."

"It would be nice to have a sister. I desperately wanted Mike to be a girl." Chelsea grinned sheepishly. "I cried when Dad told me we had a new baby brother."

"Sisters aren't always that great." Roxie made a face. "You should've heard Faye cry today when she found out it wasn't a school day. And Lacy! No boy asked her to go out tonight and she thinks her life is terrible."

"I wonder what it's like to go out with a boy." Chelsea closed her eyes and sighed dreamily. "I don't mean just sit with him at the school cafeteria or be his partner at a Sunday school party." She clasped her hands to her heart. "How would it feel to go somewhere together, just the two of you?"

Hannah shivered. "I'd be sooo nervous! What do you say to a boy?"

"Just things like we say to boys all the time." Kathy lifted herself on a high stool and rested her chin in her hands. "Like I talk to Brody Vangaar or Roxie to Rob McCrea."

Roxie giggled and nudged Kathy in the arm. "Like you talk to Roy Marks."

Kathy blushed.

"Maybe it'll be different when we're sixteen. Maybe it'll be harder to know what to say." Chelsea pushed back her red hair and looked thoughtful.

"Not for you, Chel." Roxie giggled. "You almost always know what to say and when to say it."

Chelsea grinned. "Are you saying I talk too much?"

Before anyone could answer, Chelsea's mom called down the stairs, "Kesha's here."

"Be right up, Mom." Chelsea turned to the Best Friends. "I'll go get her and bring her down. When we get to the bottom of the stairs we'll all yell, 'SURPRISE!'"

The Best Friends smiled in agreement.

Chelsea ran upstairs to the kitchen where Mom and Kesha were talking. Kesha wore a big gray T-shirt and red baggy shorts. "Hi, Kesha."

She smiled happily. "Hi. I was just telling your mom that Mrs. Murphy called this morning and said she wanted to see me. I told her I'd be here, so she's coming over after a while." Kesha turned back to Chelsea's mom. "Is that all right?"

"Of course. I'll let you know when she gets here."

"Thanks."

"See you later, Mom." Chelsea led Kesha toward the basement stairs. "Maybe Mrs. Murphy wants you to work for her again."

Kesha stopped at the basement door and caught Chelsea's hand. "I *know* something's going on." She shivered. "I just wish I knew what."

Chelsea's heart lurched. Was there something going on? "I guess you'll find out when she gets here. Let's go downstairs and play."

"It's really nice outside. Let's sit in your backyard or go to the park."

Chelsea grinned. "Maybe later. First come downstairs with me. I want to show you something."

Smiling, Kesha shrugged. She looked closer at Chelsea. "What's going on? I see you're up to something!"

Chelsea laughed and led Kesha downstairs. At

the bottom of the steps all the Best Friends yelled, "SURPRISE!"

Kesha's eyes grew big and round. She clasped her hands over her mouth and looked at the balloons, the cake, and the gifts.

Chelsea walked Kesha toward the Best Friends who were standing near the kitchen nook. "We're having a surprise party for you."

Kesha's eyes filled with tears, but she quickly brushed them away. "I never had a party before. Not ever! It's not even my birthday or anything." She looked around the rec room and gasped. "You got a big-screen TV! And a pool table and a Ping-Pong table! Chel Sea, this is totally awesome!"

Later Chelsea sat Kesha on a cushion in the middle of the floor with her gifts, and they all sat facing her.

Kesha gingerly touched the present closest to her. "Shall I open it? The paper's too beautiful!"

"Open all of them," Chelsea said smiling. She couldn't wait to see the look on Kesha's face when she saw the gifts.

Kesha opened the first package. It was from Kathy. Kesha gasped as she held up a matching skirt and blouse. "Oh my!"

"You can wear it tomorrow to church," Kathy said, looking pleased.

"I don't know what to say!" Kesha carefully put the skirt and blouse down and picked up the next gift. It was from Hannah.

Hannah nudged Chelsea and grinned.

Kesha opened it and lifted out a red sweater and black dress pants. As she held up the pants, a red, black, and white beaded headband fell to the floor. With a glad cry Kesha picked it up and tied it around her forehead. "Oh, Hannah, it's perfect!"

Hannah flushed with pleasure.

Roxie squirmed restlessly. "Open mine! Open mine!"

Kesha giggled as she tore off the paper. Inside was a pair of jeans and a plaid button-up shirt. "Oh! Beautiful!" Kesha clutched the jeans and shirt to her and helplessly shook her head.

Chelsea laughed in delight. Seeing Kesha with the gifts was as much fun as getting presents herself.

Finally Kesha opened Chelsea's present. Inside was a pack of socks of different colors and lots of beautiful undergarments. Kesha looked at Chelsea and burst into tears. "Why are you all doing this for me? I'm nobody!"

Chelsea pushed a tissue into Kesha's hand. "You are a somebody! You're Kesha Bronski! Jesus loves you."

"Does He really?"

"Yes!"

With an unsteady hand Kesha wiped away her tears. "I want Jesus to be my friend and Savior like you said."

Chelsea's heart leaped with joy. "We'll help you pray right now if you want."

Kesha nodded.

The girls held hands in a circle, and Chelsea prayed, and then Kesha repeated, "Jesus, I'm sorry for all I've done wrong. Forgive me. I give myself to You. I want You to be my friend and Savior from now on."

The girls laughed and cried and hugged Kesha one at a time.

"You're a new Kesha now," Hannah said softly. "Jesus just gave you a new spirit and made you a new person inside."

Later, upstairs in Chelsea's bedroom, Kesha tried on all her new clothes. She left on the jeans, the plaid shirt, and the beaded headband. She looked in the full-length mirror and laughed in delight.

Chelsea stood to one side and smiled at Kesha. "You look great!"

The Best Friends all agreed.

Just then Chelsea's mom called up for Kesha. "Mrs. Murphy is here."

Kesha caught Chelsea's hand. "Please go with me to talk to her. Please!"

"I will," Chelsea said softly. "Don't be afraid. You're not alone any longer."

Kesha smiled and nodded.

Chelsea asked the Best Friends to wait for them, and then she walked Kesha to the living room where Mrs. Murphy was sitting with Mom. Mrs. Murphy stood and tucked her flowered blouse deep into her tan slacks. She smiled at Kesha.

"Did I do something wrong?" Kesha's voice broke, and she swallowed hard.

"Not at all!" Mrs. Murphy squeezed Kesha's hand. "I have something important to tell you."

"I want Chelsea and her mom to stay with me."

"That's fine." Mrs. Murphy sat on a chair across from the couch.

Chelsea's mom sat on the chair beside Mrs. Murphy, while Chelsea and Kesha sat together on the couch. Chelsea felt Kesha's tension and silently prayed for her. Kesha had been right! There was something going on!

Mrs. Murphy took a deep breath. "I spoke to your father a couple of days ago and again this morning."

Kesha stiffened. "Oh?"

"I'd heard your mother was having treatment for her alcoholism and that your family needed extra help at this time. Your dad asked someone else to take your two younger brothers until your mom is home again, and I offered to have you stay with me. If you want to, that is."

Kesha looked helplessly from Mrs. Murphy to Chelsea, then back. "Why didn't my dad tell me?"

"He said he couldn't. He wanted me to. He said he was afraid you'd run away or something."

Kesha sank back, her eyes wide. "I don't know what to say."

"Mrs. Murphy really wants you with her,"

Chelsea's mom said gently. "That's why she had the bedroom made ready."

Kesha trembled.

"You'd be closer to me," Chelsea said. "I'd like that. And you could stay with Mrs. Murphy until your mom was home again. Wouldn't you like that?"

"It's such a surprise." Kesha bit her lip. "Where's my dad now?"

"With your mom." Mrs. Murphy leaned forward and looked earnestly at Kesha. "He said he'd talk to you after I did, so that if it doesn't work out with me, he can find somewhere else for you to stay."

"Why can't I stay with my big sisters and brother?"

"Because you need an adult to take care of you," Mrs. Murphy said. "It's not right for you to have to take on the responsibility for yourself at your age. You should be a child a little longer."

"She's right," Chelsea's mom said, smiling. "I wouldn't want Chelsea to be on her own. She could manage, but why should she have to? You could make it too, but why shouldn't you have the extra love and attention Mrs. Murphy can give you?"

"I wanted to meet you from the time my son first told me about you and Chelsea. When I first heard about you, you touched my heart. I prayed for a way to get to know you and help you, and God answered my prayer."

Kesha slowly smiled. "I guess I'll stay with you. I never had a bedroom to myself before."

"Maybe Chelsea can spend the night sometime."

"I'd love it!" Chelsea turned to Mom. "May I?"

"Sure." Mom stood and beckoned to Chelsea. "Let's go out and give Kesha and Mrs. Murphy time alone."

Chelsea squeezed Kesha's hand. "We'll wait in the backyard for you."

Kesha nodded. "We still have cake to eat."

"You're right! We'll let you cut it. It's your cake, you know." Chelsea squeezed Kesha's hand again and then followed Mom out of the room.

Later Chelsea stood in the backyard with the Best Friends and told them everything. They were as happy as she was for Kesha. That's what Best Friends were like. They shared the good times and the bad.

Just then Kesha called, "Chel Sea!"

"We're right here, Kesha!" Chelsea ran to meet Kesha with the Best Friends beside her. They all gathered around Kesha and listened to her talk.

Chelsea's heart filled with happiness. Friends listened and shared in each other's excitement. When Kesha finally stopped talking, Chelsea said, "It's time to eat the cake."

Kesha's dark eyes sparkled. "I'll cut us each a huge piece!"

Laughing, Chelsea led the way to the special rec room.

You are invited to become a Best Friends Member!

In becoming a member you'll receive a club membership card with your name on the front and a list of the Best Friends and their favorite Bible verses on the back along with a space for your favorite Scripture. You'll also receive a colorful, 2-inch, specially-made I'M A BEST FRIEND button and a write-up about the author, Hilda Stahl, with her autograph. As a bonus you'll get an occasional newsletter about the upcoming BEST FRIENDS books.

All you need to do is mail your NAME, ADDRESS (printed neatly, please), AGE and $3.00 for postage and handling to:

BEST FRIENDS
P.O. Box 96
Freeport, MI 49325

WELCOME TO THE CLUB!

(Authorized by the author, Hilda Stahl)